Bustah *and* Bumpah

A Tale of Two Whales

Ken Buckley

North
Country
Press

Bustah and Bumpah

ISBN 978-1-943424-12-2

Library of Congress Control Number: 2016944114

North Country Press
Unity, Maine

For my grandson Michael

and my wife Elaine, for her indefatigable support

Foreword

Although this story was inspired by an actual incident in Maine, the story is entirely fictional. With the exception of Maine place names and historical events of the era, characters and events are entirely the products of the author's imagination.

They're Here

A thick, brown blanket of dust swallowed Christine Alley, as she desperately dug her heel into the sandy gravel stretch of narrow causeway leading to Mollusk Point Lighthouse.

Amazed, she just stared as she stood between the wheels and handlebars of her blue and white Schwinn bicycle.

There was a cough and a "Wow," heard from behind, as a coughing and spluttering Karl Bunker became entangled in his own bike.

"Glad you're not on the main road," Karl said squinting through the dust.

"Look," Christine said.

"Wow. Over there!" Karl coughed and rubbed dirt out of his eyes. He cupped a hand over his forehead, squinting against the burning glare of the sun as it bounced off the glistening lamp glass. His eyes followed the tip of her finger, which pointed out beyond Mollusk Point's peppermint candy stick lighthouse.

Chest-high waves crashed below the lighthouse. White-topped waves sent sheets of foam thundering and spattering over glistening gray rocks. The waves sucked back the foam, hissing over the rocks as tangles of brown kelp and dark green seaweed swirled angrily, like Medusa's tresses.

"See?" Christine excitedly grabbed Karl's arm. "Over there, just this side of Islesboro."

"Looks like whales."

"Looks like? What else could they be? Look! There they go!" The two whales showed off their white bellies, waved their flukes, dived, and then spouted two white fountains through their blow holes.

Quickly, she dusted off her arms, flicked the dust off her white blouse, and pulled up her bike. Standing on the pedals, she furiously raced toward the lighthouse at the end of the narrow path of the rock-flanked premonitory.

"Come on," she cried back to Karl.

"Hold on! Give me a second!"

But she was already alongside the keeper's house. It was a story-and-a-half white structure with a red metal roof with a white picket fence that draws a triangle around the oil house and storage barn.

"Nettie?" Christine called, stepping over her fallen bike. A tall, lean, sprightly Nettie Beal flung open the screen door, gripping a handful of letters.

"Are you okay? What happened?" she asked, her eyes scanning the kids' faces, her glasses now dangling on her blouse from a gold-flecked black cord.

"Whales...whales!" Christine beamed; charging up the broad wooden steps beneath the gold painted hand-carved sign: *Mollusk Point Post Office Me.*

Nettie's steel blue eyes widened with a smile, as she pressed the letters against her breast.

"Oh, my Lord," she said, spinning around.

"They'll be level with the point soon," Karl said, running up the steps.

"Let's go watch from the tower," Nettie said, dashing through the door. "I should have this mail sorted, but, it can wait. Come on."

Dropping the mail on a table behind the wall of metallic gold-trimmed mailboxes, she snatched a flowered head scarf, twirled and knotted it, and headed for the side door with both kids racing to keep up.

Nettie's sneakers slapped the concrete walkway, her brisk short steps echoing along the corridor which linked the house with the lighthouse entry door.

2

She shot up three stone steps and lifted the heavy black metal cross latch as if it were a matchstick. Gripping the handle, the heavy door's rubber seal gave a slight pop as she slowly pulled it open.

All three gasped as they stepped into the wide circular base of the lighthouse and the dry concrete air brushed by them. Without hesitation, they strode across the floor to a flight of black metal steps with a handrail circling the inner wall and disappearing into the turret.

"I wonder—" Nettie started. "It must be—" Her voice rumbled back around the stairwell.

"What?" asked Christine, who was right behind her.

Nettie pressed on until she finally reached a small landing and another door leading to the lookout deck.

"Has to be. Betcha it has to be," she painted her face an apple blush.

A puzzled Christine looked at Karl, shrugged her shoulders and helped push the heavy metal door open.

Its rusty creak was overwhelmed by the noise of a lobster boat revving up at the end of a string of traps just off the rocks below.

"Oh, look! There they are!" Christine said. "They're almost here!"

The three of them gripped the iron railing, gazing in wonder as the whales majestically surfaced and dove theatrically as though they knew they were being watched.

Nettie, as excited as she was, was unable to give the show her full attention. Her neck strained around the light, as she intently followed a white and brown-trimmed lobster boat bobbing and sputtering as the stern man unconcernedly plunged his hands into a smelly barrel of oily herring heads and tails. Quickly, he scooped a handful out of the thick brown soup into a bait bag, tightened the strings, and just as quickly, hung it inside the trap.

A concerned Nettie peered around the glass turret. Her eyes stared hard at the boat, then back at the whales, slightly more than a stone's throw from the rocks.

Christine started to yell and wave.

"Over here! Here we are!" she shouted, waving her arms as she jumped up and down.

"Stop! Stop that immediately." Nettie's anxious face was but an inch from Christine's as she waved her hands urging her to quiet down.

"What's the matter?" Christine asked, looking scared and pulling back, her voice trembling.

Nettie shook her head and reached for Christine's hands. "I'm sorry," she said, pulling the girl toward her. "You shouldn't wave at them. I'm sorry—I didn't mean to shake you up. I'll explain. I don't want them to come too close."

The kids swapped puzzled looks. Karl shrugged his shoulders, his palms upturned. Christine's brow furrowed, her mouth fell slightly ajar. She had never seen Nettie so erratic.

The lobster boat roared again as it leveled with a yellow and red-tipped buoy, the helmsman deftly hooking it. Looping the cord over the pulley block, he took two quick loops around a capstan just below the wheel, set the buoy aside, eased a toggle bottle alongside it, and curled the rope on deck.

A wooden-lathed trap exploded from the surface, water streaming from it and alive with thrashing lobsters and a large cod fish. Laying it on the gunwale, the stern man unlooped the trap door, pulled out the lobsters, and dropped them into a plastic container. The helmsman took one, measured it with a copper metal rule, and flung it back into the sea. The cod was unceremoniously plopped into another wooden keep crate.

"There. You've got your lobsters and fish for the cat, now get on with ya' and get out of here," Nettie said with a growl, as she continued to spy around the lamp house, and gave an even more anxious look toward the whales. Both chubby whales hooted as they happily shot jets of water out of their blow holes.

"Don't let them see you," she said, staring at the whales, as Karl and Christine looked at each other bewildered.

"Oh, look at ya' my lovelies...you've grown so big. Now be good and listen to ya' mommy - don't come any closer..." Nettie's voice was just a whisper, almost like a child's. A plea amid the thundering roll of breakers and screeching of gulls circling and diving for treats tossed by the stern man.

"Listen," she said. A shrill whistle, followed by squeaks and even higher-pitched whistles cut through the cries of the gulls. Then, they heard a clicker-clacker sound, like a wooden stick being dragged along fence palings.

"Oh, are they happy to be back. Listen to them," Nettie said, the tiny cheeks of her narrow face puffed into a round smile. The trumpeting and honks continued, along with the clicker-clacker and toy-flute whistles.

Christine and Karl looked dumbfounded as Nettie Beal crouched down suspiciously, stealing a look around the glistening glass and chrome tower.

Both chuckled and Nettie turned her head, and pressed a finger to her bottom lip with a cautionary, "Sssh."

The two ducked their heads and came up behind Nettie Beal.

"Ah, yes, I know. I know what you're up to," she said, as her shoulders shuddered beneath her red plaid hunting shirt.

The two white whales continued rolling and splashing, shooting up jets of water, and cavorting like two oversized kids at play.

"Look," said Christine, jumping up and wildly waving her arms.

"Stop—for heaven's sake, child. Whad ya think you're doing?" Nettie said desperately. "Oh my gosh! If they see you, they'll have their guns out in no time."

"Oh, I'm sorry, I forgot," Christine said, with her hands pressed against her face.

Karl peeped around the globe. The lobstermen were enjoying the sight too. The helmsman stood by the davit with

5

one hand on the hoist shaking his head admiringly, whilst the sternman stared, dangling a bait bag in one hand, while the other rested on the rim of the large wooden bait barrel.

"I hope they go away," Nettie said. "Go on. Go away!" she said, shooing them away desperately with her hands. She leaned back, and mouthed a silent prayer.

As if by magic, the boat's engine roared and a belch of black smoke bellowed out of the rusty exhaust above the cabin. The helmsman spun the wheel, and followed a string of bobbing buoys, but he couldn't take his eyes off the whales. He jerked a thumb in their direction and yelled to his sternman, who stretched his arms and rested his hands on the cabin roof.

Nettie Beal slowly slid her back down the glass dome, slumping on the deck beside the kids.

"Thank God. Oh, goodness," she said, thoroughly spent and puffing through her lips.

"Never seen whales so close before," Karl said.

"Me, either," said Christine.

"Yes, and that's a problem," Nettie said, straightening up staring after the lobster boat.

The kids exchanged puzzled glances as they leaned over the rail, absorbed by the show of the whales.

"Go away! Oh, go away!"

Christine and Karl gripped the rail as they watched Nellie intently.

"Shoo," she half-whispered.

"Do you really think they'd kill them?" Christine asked.

Nettie Beal grimly nodded her head.

"But, why?" Christine said.

Nettie Beal shook her head, shrugged her shoulders, and hopelessly spread her palms.

"Why? I don't know…I don't honestly know the answers to a lot of puzzling things in this world. But I know one thing—I swear by it, too. No one had better touch those whales! It would be like shooting a dog, a cat, a cow—"

6

Her voice trailed off.

Christine clasped Nettie's hand gripping the hand rail.

"You really love them, don't you?" she said, her eyes bubbling with warmth.

"I do, I love them," she said, a smile lighting up her face as she turned to Christine, clasping both of her hands in hers. "That's why I want them to leave. I want them to go before they get shot and butchered."

"Are you sure?" Karl asked. "But, who would do that?"

"Them! Those fishermen! They'd do it. Or anyone else with a gun."

"But what would they do with a dead whale?" Karl asked. "My dad's a lobsterman and he wouldn't shoot one."

Nettie's face was drawn tight.

"Please don't talk like that. Please."

"My dad's a lobsterman, too," said Christine. "But if he ever thought—ever thought—of doing it, there'd be big trouble in our house. My mom wouldn't stand for it either."

"Your dad's a buyer. He's not a lobsterman," Karl said.

"A lobster buyer. So? There's not much difference, is there? One catches the other buys and sells. They're both in the lobster business."

Nettie smiled, linking her arms around their shoulders.

"Come on now, let's not fight amongst ourselves. We have to stand together and make sure these whales are safe."

They must have stayed there for an hour, standing, sitting, watching, listening, and laughing as the whales called to each other across the white tops.

"I think they're trying to tell us something," Christine said.

Nettie smiled and nodded her head.

Karl stared straight across the water.

"They're like submarines, only smoother," he said, as the whales continued their show.

Then, just as suddenly as they had appeared, they quickly disappeared beneath a choppy stretch of bluish green water.

Nettie stood up, her face a mixture of worry and happiness.

"They must have heard you," Christine said.

"Hopefully," Nettie nodded, and then shook her head glumly. "It's a rotten shame that everything beautiful—like those whales, and birds, deer—oh, I don't know," she said despondently. "Come on. Let's have something to eat."

Karl clattered down the metal stairs behind Christine, as Nettie followed.

In the kitchen, Nettie served her famous lettuce and tomato sandwiches topped with a generous spoonful of creamy mayonnaise.

While Karl and Christine ate, Nettie was up and down, crossing the kitchen to the windows that framed the tower and sea.

"I was just thinking," she said, sitting down next to the kids. "I wonder if they knew what I was thinking."

Christine stopped chewing and looked at Nettie. "I wonder."

"Oh, come on, now. Surely you don't think—"

"Why not?" said Christine. "Animals and mammals have this strange ability to communicate."

Karl chuckled.

"Well, they do. Sometimes it seems like Tom understands me, even when I don't feel good."

"Your cat knows when you call him. They all do that— cats, dogs—when you call. They're used to it," Karl said, with a shrug of his shoulders.

"Then, why not whales?" Christine said, staring hard at Karl. Nettie beamed.

As they talked excitedly about whales and animals and their means of communication, Nettie picked up a photo frame holding three head shots of men in Coast Guard uniforms.

"Phil and the boys would have loved to have been here today," Nettie said, proudly looking at the men's pictures.

"You must really miss Phil." Christine said.

Nettie nodded her head.

"Been gone for a year, but I still miss him," she said, kissing the pictures and placing the frame on the table. "My Phil. If it hadn't been for him, I wouldn't have been able to take over as keeper."

"And Richard and Harold?" asked Karl.

"Richard's on the *Kennebec* at Southwest Harbor, and Harold's training recruits in Connecticut," Nettie said, a touch of pride swelling her voice. "They're both good boys, and they love the sea and everything that's in it – just like Phil."

With a final urgent message of caution about keeping the whale visit secret, Nettie waved from the porch as the kids pushed off down the causeway, a narrow neck of land that ran back into Quarry Cove, with their fists clenched around both mail and handlebars.

Pledge of Silence

Clusters of pine, cedar and silver birch trees, with their branches creaking and swaying and leaves waving, sprung up between the fishing shacks and Chuddy Spooner's half-painted boat storage shed on Quarry Cove Hill. Dinghies and lobster boats lazily tugged at their buoys.

Just beyond lay non-navigable Rocky Marsh, with its century-old skeletal remains of *Selena's Wish*, a rum-running Schooner. Dried seaweed, sea moss, and kelp dangled like long uncombed tresses from the weathered gray bones of its hull.

Some tourists would cut out of traffic and nose into a tiny parking lot with its bench and sign marking Rocky Marsh Preserve. As Bangor and Belfast traffic zoomed past, shutters snapped, kids played, while others just stood and stared at the crumbling relic.

The cove resembled a long tablespoon. The narrow handle divided Quarry Hill from Mollusk Point breakwater and lighthouse. Except for gales, tides gently rose and fell along the handle into the rock-protected cove. Thanks to fresh water cascading over a dam from Spooner's Pond, the cove was almost always full, but a real low tide tested the best navigation skills of lobstermen, who lived in a small cluster of white framed homes on the side of Quarry Cove Hill. Beyond the cove's iron bridge, it was barely a shift into second gear where Route 1A suddenly swerved past a large parking lot for Breaker Point Lookout.

Huge white crested rollers would roar up and over the Lookout's grayish-red rocks, scattering seagulls and tourists alike. Gulls defiantly screeched as they soared high over the point before swooping down to find a treat tossed by a tourist.

And, just about any time on any given day, motorists would fill the terraced parking lot. Many would just stand in awe, as seven- and eight-foot waves hurtled against the rocks. Nature painted an even wilder scene in fall. Seas driven by southern hurricanes tested the metal of sightseers. Over the years two or three seeking the best holiday photo and ignoring the *WARNING- HIGH SEAS* had been pulled out to sea and lost.

After snapping pictures, eating lunch, or daringly dodging waves and catching some spray, the motorists would happily climb back into their cars and trucks and either head down to Belfast or up to Bangor.

Pepper Mill, off Route 1A, where Christine lived, was tucked behind Dingle's Rock, a huge granite mountain nestled between two small hills. It was named after Charlie Dingle, a stone cutter, who opened and ran the first quarry.

Quarry Hill Cove and Pepper Mill Village were two very different, very small, and barely known towns. Unless you lived there, or knew someone who did, they were typical rustic New England villages of the early 1940s and before. Little, if anything, had changed since then.

Riding home from the lighthouse, Christine braked and Karl almost collided with her bike's rear fender.

"Hope I'm not on the road when you get your license," he said.

"I'll have mine before you," Christine said, looking back along the causeway.

Nettie Beal was still waving from atop the steps of the keeper's red, tin-roofed cottage.

"I think she's going loopy," said Karl.

"Don't say that. She's a lovely person," Christine said.

"I like her. But my dad says living alone is no good for anyone."

"But Phil's only been gone a year," Christine said.

"Long enough. She should have found someone else by now."

"And I suppose your dad said that, too?" Christine said.

"Yeah," Karl said, nodding his head.

"Is he going to tell you how to think?" Christine said with her feet firmly planted on each side of her bike. "My daddy says this, and my daddy thinks that. Is that how you're going to plow through life?"

"Oh, come on, it was just about Nettie."

"And, what if he thinks that you and I shouldn't be seen together, eh? What about that? Is that the end?"

"Of course not, honest. I'd never break up with you just because dad told me to," Karl said, his face sullen.

"We'll see."

She pressed on the pedal and rolled off toward the bridge. Karl followed her, until she braked.

"And another thing. Don't you dare tell anyone—especially your daddy or anyone else—about the whales, or else."

"I won't. But my dad wouldn't shoot a whale."

"Don't be so sure. You heard what Nettie said about men and guns."

"Oh, she just got carried away."

Christine's eyes narrowed into her taut face. "You've changed. I don't know whether I can take much more of this."

"But Chrissie…believe me…I mean…I'm not telling Dad. I wouldn't."

Her face relaxed in a warm smile, but her eyes puzzled him. They weren't blue, or brown. They had a soft, yet sparkling silver glow that could focus into a penetrating stare as they did just then.

"I'll have nothing to do with you ever. Ever! I mean it."

They were chums since kindergarten. They'd kidded and feigned love, not really knowing what love was, but an overpowering mystical aura—which left Karl completely befuddled. They'd started with daring and embarrassing quick pecks on the cheek, until one afternoon at Lookout Point, with the surf rolling and sighing as it fanned out and sputtered across the rocks, Christine had kissed him differently.

It was a warm, soft, gentle kiss on his lips. He tasted the brine on her lips, while inhaling her sweet fragrance. He sensed an overpowering resoluteness and pureness. They were twelve at that time, and from that moment on they shared an unspoken adoration for each other. It was a love that neither one of them had expressed, except for a kiss, a hug, and holding hands. And, it was a love that would remain a secret, like so many other things they shared.

Now they had another secret.

He reached for her hand. Christine placed her hand in his and leaned over, planting a soft kiss squarely on his surprised mouth. He melted. He never knew when she would do it, and it always sent a meteoric thrill through his body.

"Promise," he said, his voice squeaking. He coughed, clearing his throat trying to deepen his voice. Christine hid a smile.

"Chocolate syrup," she said, nodding toward the muddy cove. "Good. That means they won't come up here," she said, cautiously crossing Route 1A.

"See ya," she called, waving from the other side, as the cars and trucks streaked by.

Secret's Out

"Dad, would you ever kill a whale?"

"Depends." Seth Bunker spooned out some potatoes and passed the bowl across the kitchen table to Karl. "Dig in, get some meat on them bones."

"But would you?" Karl asked, slicing a carrot, and licking a finger as he took the gravy bowl from his mother.

"Like a fella says, it depends."

"On what?"

Seth Bunker's cheeks ballooned with a mouthful of potato. "So how come you're so interested in whales?"

"Eh…school. Yeah, we're studying whales."

"You can't kid me, son. You saw them two white whales dancing off Mollusk Point this afternoon, didn't ya?" His hands firmly gripped his knife and fork on both sides of his plate as he stared, eyebrows raised, a whimsical smile creasing his cheeks, still chewing.

"How did you know?

"Oh, I heard Harry and Todd Hawkins yakking about it on the radio. I was out on the other side of Deadman's Point."

"You see them?" asked Karl's mom, Laura.

"Oh, yeah. They were fantastic! Leaping and diving, they were having a great—"

"That's good, as long as they stay away from the lobsters," Seth Bunker said, his cheeks puffed as he munched noisily away.

"But what if—"

Seth Bunker set the heels of his knife and fork on each side of his plate. "They're up here for one purpose—to feed on everything we make a living from, just like the seals eating our herring. There's something more to 'em than just entertaining people."

"So what are you going to do?" Karl asked, as his father continued to shovel potatoes into an already full mouth.

A frown swept across his father's brow, his eyes narrowed. "Get rid of 'em—that's what we'll do."

A shocked Karl dropped his knife and fork and pushed away from the table staring horrified at his dad.

"You...you can't do that..." he said, as his mother pulled back, surprised at her son's retort.

"Oh, I forgot something," Karl said, jumping up from the table.

"Come and eat your supper," his mom cried out. But he was on his bike, out of the yard, his feet off the pedals as he coasted downhill toward the bridge.

Horns blared and a truck driver yelled as he flew across 1A, head hunched over the handlebars. He swirled around Dingle's Rock and pedaled furiously past the silver birch and the cloud-scratching cedar and maple trees down Pepper Mill Road all the way into Pepper Mill village.

Where'd They Go?

Christine slammed the cottage screen door behind her and raced toward him over the brick path that threaded itself between two giant red rhododendrons.

"So they know?" she said, angrily shaking her head, and muttering something he couldn't hear.

"I didn't say a word," Karl said, hands raised nervously in front of him.

"We've got to let Nettie know." She spun around, staring hard at him, her sharp steel gray eyes cutting through him.

"I didn't say a word…not a word…honest…I didn't," Karl said, anxiously shifting from one foot to the other. "Don't you believe me?"

Christine's face was ashen. "Won't be long before everyone knows, you can bet on that. No secrets around here, that's for sure. Everyone knows everything sometimes before you know it yourself."

"Huh?" Karl said, confusedly shaking his head. But she ignored him.

They pedaled their bikes back up Pepper Mill hill, dodged horn-tooting traffic across 1A, turned right past the iron bridge onto Mollusk Point causeway and raced toward the lighthouse.

"I knew it," Nettie said, angrily pacing up and down across the cottage kitchen. "Now, you know what'll be next?"

"But they've gone…haven't they?" Karl said.

"For now, but I bet they're not too far away."

"I'm sorry," Christine said. "I should never have waved—"

"You're not to blame, Chrissie," Nettie said, spinning on her heel and laying a comforting hand on Christine's shoulder.

"Karl's dad is already oiling his rifle," Christine said sharply. "I suppose the rest of the Quarry Cove crowd will be downing beer and whiskey in Spooner's bait house before long, getting ready to attack."

"Well, they hunt everything else—deer, bear, raccoons, rabbits, moose—and anything and everything else that has fur on it. So why not whales?" Nettie said, angrily shaking her head.

"But whales don't have fur. I mean—" Karl shook his head and chuckled. "Whoops, should not have said that."

"These are the Beluga whales," Nettie said, marching across the kitchen with an open encyclopedia in her hands.

"It's spring, time for them to forage for food close to shore, and enter cold estuaries–just like the one that runs between Quarry Cove and this causeway," she said taking a great breath, and emphasizing each sentence as she wagged her right index finger.

Karl and Christine listened intently, as Nettie paced back and forth reading passages aloud from the bulky book.

"These whales are friendly," she said. "Let's hope they've gone before they become too friendly around here." Her hands folded the book shut with a muffled thud. "I know they're friendly—Lord, I know only too well how friendly they are." She firmly planted her hands on her hips and stared out through the side window past the lighthouse.

It was almost nine before they finished the last lettuce and cucumber sandwich. Nettie confidently placed her arms around their shoulders and walked them toward the door.

"Keep your eyes and ears open, and let me know the moment—the instant—the instant you hear anything." Then, with a finger against her lips, she said, "Sssh," and they shot off, peddling wildly down Mollusk Point Causeway.

"I'm scared," Christine said, as she braked with her heel at the iron bridge.

"But they've gone, haven't they? There's nothing to worry about?"

17

"I don't think they have. I heard them when we entered the cottage."

"But you never said anything. I didn't hear a thing."

"Yeah. Clickety-click-clickety they went, just like a cricket, only louder."

"I thought that was a cricket. And, another thing, I thought all whales are black."

"Belugas are white," Christine said, mounting her bike. "See ya in the morning—and don't forget." She braked again. "Now don't you dare say anything to anyone at school. Promise?"

Traffic was still zipping along 1A as she looked for an opening, and then deftly maneuvered between a truck loaded with chickens and a semitrailer with *Alley's Fresh Maine Lobster – Shipped Anywhere* painted in huge red letters with a big red boiled lobster hovering over *Alley* in the rear corner of the trailer. The driver hooted and waved, and Christine waved back.

Karl watched, and then sped across the road. "You don't believe me, do you?"

"I'm okay, you don't have to follow me," Christine said, as he drew level with her.

"I'll ride with you," he said. Christine lowered her head and pedaled furiously around Dingle's Rock, now circled by a crimson sun that trimmed the clouds with gold.

Winded, Karl caught up with her as she leaned the bike against the house. She blew him a kiss, and snapped the screen door behind her.

5

They're Back

His dad's boat was puttering out of the cove when he dashed downstairs into the kitchen Monday morning. He downed a dish of corn flakes and took a quick gulp of coffee as his mother sat staring concernedly at the radio on the counter by the window.

"...conditions continue to grow worse in Korea as rumors of Soviet tanks moving closer to the 38th Parallel..."

"What's that all about?" Karl said, munching on a piece of toast, his book satchel dangling from his other hand, ready to run.

"Looks like we're going to have another war," Laura Bunker said, an exasperated look clouding her face.

"Korea? Where's that?"

"Oh, I don't know. But we're just barely out of one, and we're into another one."

He dashed out of the house past his worried mother and ran down the small hill toward the bridge. Then he stopped dead in his tracks by a large rock that overlooked the cove.

The excitement was electrifying. Kids were yelling, screaming, and jumping with delight. A throng of kids in a jumble of apple red and pumpkin orange jackets and coats were draped over the bridge rail in the parking lot off Route 1A.

He looked again. Two unmistakable short jets of brownish water and two white snouts bobbing near the bridge, unleashed even more wild cheers and yells, just as Elwood Tinker's yellow school bus Number 2 squeaked to a stop behind the cheering kids. Elwood quickly hopped down the bus steps and sprinted to the railing.

Karl's ears thundered as his sneakers pounded into the ground. "Oh, my God…" A combination of fear and excitement clutched his heart as he raced toward the bridge.

Christine was running across the bridge toward him as a big splash brought even more delighted cheers from the crowd.

Briefly they stared at each other. Then, they gripped the iron rail and stared unbelievably as the Belugas happily dived, rolled, and cavorted. The air was filled with kids yelling and whales trumpeting, snorting, and even whistling, with an occasional…*clickity-clickity-clack-click.*

"There. I told you. See," Christine said, looking quickly at Karl and back at the cove which looked like the inside of a washing machine on full spin.

"Holy smoke," said Karl. "Wow…this is great…just great! Ain't never seen anything like this before…"

A splash of water sent a wave up over the bridge rail and cut him off from what he was about to say. Both yelled and jumped back, but not quickly enough, and got soaked.

They both laughed at each other. Christine let out a yell of surprise as she shook her shoulders and looked at her sodden blouse, skirt, and sneakers. Karl was roaring with laughter. Drenched, he continued to laugh uncontrollably, as another delighted roar from below and a splash sent another wave spattering over the rail as Christine's hands frantically tried to brush off the water.

"I'm soaked," she cried out. "Soaked!"

Karl roared as a *clickety-clack* sounded from a happy whale below.

"Oh, look Christine," he said, leaning over the railing staring down at two plump white whales leaning back, flippers waggling, with waves from their boisterous activity rocking lobster boats and skiffs, bobbing like corks in the cove.

"I'm soaking and all you can—"

She ran back to the rail and stared dumbfounded at the two whales.

"Oh…oh…oh…how lovely!" She hooked onto Karl's forearm, her face wreathed in happiness.

"This is fantastic…I can't believe it…I just—"

The two whales did a quick nose dive accompanied by a thunderous splash. Christine yelled, but it was too late. She looked at Karl and he looked at her, both soaked to the skin, and they both doubled over with laughter.

The two whales surfaced and leaned back with big grins that stretched across their snouts. The kids by the parking lot roared with laughter, yelling and calling for them to dive. Karl and Christine got ready to jump back as the larger of the two whales did a quick back roll letting out an air horn roar as if to show his or her appreciation for the crowd's attention. The smaller whale did a *clickety-clack* and dived after the other. The crowd roared with approval.

"They're laughing," Christine said, as the whales surfaced and reclined facing the crowd. "Look at them—their eyes…oh what beautiful faces and eyes…they're laughing!" She looked at Karl. Both laughed as eight hundred pounds of whale nearly lifted out of the water and crashed back into the cove. Small waves surged across the cove, rocking boats and splashing on the rocks, as the kids screamed with delight.

Christine pulled at Karl's shirt sleeve.

"Look," she said, nodding toward the parking area across the bridge. The black and white Pepper Mill & Quarry Cove Police Department cruiser with two roof-mounted red lights had drawn alongside the school bus. Kids turned and stared as the town's sole patrolman, Officer Joe Mullins, stretched his short torso out of the cruiser. Seeing the crowd, he tucked his chin into his neck, eyes flicking side to side.

The kids stared harder at him, chuckling and nudging each other to draw attention to him as he bunched his shoulders, bowed his arms affectedly like a gunslinger, and strode down to the fence. His hips rolled awkwardly as he sucked in his beer paunch. His right hand hovered above a black holster, which held his Smith & Wesson Thirty-Eight.

"Come on—quick!" Christine tore off, her school bag half dragging behind her.

Together they elbowed up to the rail next to Mullins who had already unsnapped the holster strap holding his pistol.

"What are you going to do?" Christine said, with her horrified face only inches from the red-cheeked patrolman.

Mullins' forehead furrowed like a plowed field, his jaws rolling as if he was chewing gum. Giving her a brief glance, he looked straight ahead, grinned, and nodded toward the whales.

"They'd better get back to where they came 'afore low tide," he said, his fingers impatiently tapping the hammer on his pistol, while the other hand gripped the rail.

"What if they don't?" Christine asked anxiously as she stared at the middle-aged policeman's puffy face and down at his pistol.

"They may have to tow them back to sea," Mullins said. "Then again, if they get stranded in the mud—well, there ain't much we can do, say, except…shoot 'em."

"Nooooo!" Christine screamed. The parking lot went silent. Even the whales appeared to have heard her scream, and waited. The crowd of kids around her suddenly turned and stared as Mullins drew back. He was shocked and raised his palms toward Christine.

"You can't do that," Karl said.

"Do what?" Lorraine McDonald, a classmate asked, stepping forward.

"Didn't say I was…just said maybe."

Tripper Gleason, Pepper Mill High's all-star linebacker, grudgingly shoved his big-boned frame to the fore.

"Betcha I could nail 'em with my thirty ought six, Joe," he said, a grin stretching across his pugnacious pimpled face.

"Over my dead body," Christine determinedly snapped back, her face almost nose to nose with his.

"Mine too," Karl snapped, glaring at the linebacker.

"Couple of toughies, eh?" Gleason scoffed at them.

"I've got a twenty-two," Karl said, raising a finger at Gleason. "I'll have that out too, and I won't be shooting at whales."

Her face beaming, Christine scrunched up next to Karl, gripping his arm, her fists trembling.

"Hey, now lookey here, this ain't Dodge City. We don't want any of that around here," Joe Mullins said, raising both palms in front of him and looking sharply at Karl.

"Well, he'd better watch it—or else."

Mullins swallowed hard and nodded his head at Elwood Tinker. "You'd better get aboard that bus if you're going to school, 'cause he's leaving."

Tinker raised his palm to Mullins and trotted over to the bus.

"Come on you guys if you want a ride to school. Come on. We're late already."

Up and around Dingle's Rock, then down a steep bank past the long tree- and camp-lined Duck Lake, past Christine's house, and all the way into Pepper Mill, Gleason leered over the back of his seat muttering and teasing Karl and Christine, while his toadies pressed forward grinning and laughing. But the bus hummed with excited talk about the whales. Even Tinker was delightedly expressing his enthusiasm with the kids.

Clash at School

"Watch them. Take pictures, but don't interfere," Principal Laura Brown said from behind the podium on the stage in Pepper Mill High School auditorium. "The authorities know what to do. Leave it to them." With that, she twisted her narrow figure, flipped back a lock of red hair, and brusquely left the stage.

"Yeah—we know," Christine said with a snort. "Shoot them."

"That jerk isn't going to shoot them, I know that," Karl said, sidestepping and dodging students as Christine marched briskly ahead of him into the brown wood-stained principal's office.

"This is a matter for the authorities," Principal Brown said sitting erect in her chair as the Guidance Counselor, Roger Millett, looked on seriously. "You should stay clear and not interfere."

"But Miss Brown…" Christine started.

"That's all I have to say," Laura Brown said, nodding to Millett to take over.

Millett cleared his throat as he walked toward the two students. With shiny brown shoes and a smart brown sports jacket over his razor-creased gray slacks, he could have been a bank president.

"Look, the police won't allow anyone to shoot those whales, unless—"

"Unless?" Christine anxiously snapped back at Millett in despair.

"Well, unless they become a hazard to the communities."

"How can they be a hazard? They just swam into the pool," Karl said, as Christine gripped his right hand.

"I know," said Millett. "But, you have to watch out for the safety of the community."

Karl and Christine swapped puzzled looks, shaking their heads incredulously.

Millet rested his elbows on the desk and smiled.

"It would be fine if the whales had protection—but there isn't any. They're still heavily hunted for meat and oil, especially in Japan and some other Asian countries."

"But these whales are harmless," Christine said, as Karl nodded his head in agreement.

Millet took a deep sigh, spread his palms, and stared hopelessly at the duo. "What can I say?" he said. "Whales can do a lot of damage to the fishing industries. They can gulp down a ton of herring and crustaceans with one swallow. They're not a protected species—which means, the authorities can do anything to get rid of them."

Karl and Christine stared hopelessly at each other.

Shuffling uneasily, Millett leaned forward with a determined look. "I don't know when, but I feel sure that some years from now, whales and a lot of other species will be sheltered under protective laws to guard against extinction. But," he said as he drew a deep sigh and nodded toward the calendar on the wall behind him, "certainly not in this day and age."

Christine and Karl looked at the large calendar with a full color picture of Cape Elizabeth's lighthouse, *June 1950.*

The Show Begins

That afternoon, scores of cars were packed on the shoulder of 1A next to the iron bridge. Hundreds of people pressed up against the railings on both sides of the pool, calling out to each other and trying to imitate the trumpeting and clicking sounds of the whales.

Christine grabbed Karl's hand as they elbowed, squeezed and excused their way through the throng to the rail.

The patrol car, with its red light flashing on the roof, was parked alongside 1A as Joe Mullins tooted a whistle between his lips, while waving his arms in an attempt to keep traffic moving.

"Oh, no," Christine said, as she looked down the embankment where a ring of Fish and Game Wardens and the Pepper Mill & Quarry Cove Chief of Police, Clarence "Woody" Harrington, were engaged in a feverish heart to heart with Nettie Beal, her hands wagging in front of the Chief's face as the stern game wardens looked on.

Christine vaulted the fence, with Karl right behind her running toward Nettie. An excited Nettie appreciably extended her arms, wrapping them around their shoulders.

"You'll have to stay behind the fence," the Chief said to Karl and Christine. But they didn't move. Nettie gripped them tighter.

"I'm just explaining to the Chief how he can handle this situation without any trouble," Nettie said with a smile.

"I appreciate it, Nettie, but look at the fuss this is causing."

"Give them a chance. It's not every day that two beautiful Belugas – Bustah and Bumpah – visit us."

The Chief's jaw dropped and he shook his head.

"Oh – so now they got names?"

"Why, of course, they do. They belong to a rare form of endangered whale species, and should not be touched—under federal regulations."

Mullins stared unbelievably at Nettie, and then walked up to the wardens.

"D'ya hear that? These are rare and you can't touch them," he said, cocking his thumb toward Nettie, her feet in white sneakers firmly and defiantly planted apart on the bank, and her arms around the waists of her two friends.

"Another thing, too," the Chief said, "they're called Bustah and Bumpah...eh? Ain't ever heard of whales with names like that."

The wardens looked up and grinned, then broke out laughing, except for one who pursed his lips and walked up to Nettie.

"Got any proof on that, ma'am?" he asked, a trace of a smile trying to hide behind his rugged, ridged, and sunburned face.

"Of what?" Nettie asked.

"That these two Belugas are named Bustah and Bumpah?" He sniffled a little, and chuckled.

"They're regulars – and those are their proper names. How can you possibly call someone a Beluga? Hey! Beluga! Come get your dinner!"

The chief warden laughed and shook his head. "I wasn't thinking about their names as much as that you were saying they were protected. Ya know, I don't know whether they are or not."

"Well you should...why, a man of your position. You should..."

"We're Fish and Game, ma'am, not Sea and Shore Wardens."

"Doesn't matter. Everyone—that is, everyone who knows animals and mammals knows that Belugas are an endangered species," she said contemptuously.

The chief warden's face held a faint smile as he slowly shook his head.

27

"Well, first I heard of it, ma'am. There are no restrictions on whales, any more than there are on seals."

"So, I suppose that is your justification in shooting two perfectly harmless baby whales?"

"Baby? Hey now, just a minute. Nobody's talking about shootin' 'em. At least, not yet."

"You are disgusting. Revolting," Nettie Beal said.

Turning to the crowd she shouted, "They're going to shoot those poor whales."

There was a hush. An empty, stunning silence followed, and then a reverberating murmur that grew steadily into a growl as people noisily shouted echoing the news. People started to wave their fists.

There were shouts of, "No," and, "Leave 'em alone, you killers."

The warden looked lost as Mullins stared at Nettie.

"You are going to cause a riot, if you keep that up," he started, just as two enormous smacks and roars drew everyone's attention to the center of the pool.

The crowd's protests quickly ebbed, and they let out a wild roar. Bustah and Bumpah were rolling and diving and slapping around in what was left of the tide, now on the ebb, sending up jets of muddied water, as they bellowed, almost laughing, with that unmistakable sound of clickety-click-clickety-click.

The crowd whooped and hollered on both sides of the pool. This only seemed to excite and inspire Bustah and Bumpah into performing encore upon encore.

The Chief went solemnly back to his car, and the wardens retired to their green pickups. But the crowd showed no signs of moving, but was increasing as homeward-bound motorists left their vehicles on both sides of the narrow two-lane artery.

The line of cars down each side of the narrow highway slowed to a crawl. Soon, they were barely moving despite the chief's and warden's attempts to keep a traffic lane open.

By seven o'clock, traffic was at a standstill. The enormous crowds had managed to cut across the bridge into Quarry Cove, and now lined the pool's banks, all excitedly waving across the pond and calling for the whales to surface.

Minute by minute, the ripples on the pool grew less and less, as the tide withdrew and the big, white mud-covered Bustah and the smaller brownish-red Bumpah, settled into the thick warm mud on the bottom of the pool. Bustah's big fluke wiggled above the surface as ripples of water sloshed around his melon head. Just a hint of Bumpah's head could be seen amid the brownish water, as the baby whale nestled close to his mother.

Except for an occasional flip of flukes and a flapping of their flippers, Bustah and Bumpah appeared to be settling in for the evening. With a gleam in their tiny eyes and a smile on their big, wide mouths, they dived, sending up fountains of water.

"Look! Did you see that?"

Karl looked at the whales, as they carefully raised their heads above the water. They were still chattering, giving out a click now and then.

"Their eyes," Christine said, "Look."

"Holy Toledo! They're winking!" Karl said, and she hugged his arm, laughing. Then, just as always, she planted a full kiss on his cheek.

8

Family Fracture

WBCF's News at Eleven rumbled as Police Chief Clarence "Woody" Harrington warned of major traffic problems. Pepper Mill and Quarry Cove First Selectman, Chauncey Philpot, was seen hesitatingly calling for state assistance. Somehow, Nettie managed to get in a short burst, telling the world that the whales were protected under federal law and they should be left alone.

But Clark McQuaid, a lobsterman from Pepper Mill, pompously asserted that the whales were after "his lobsters" and his brother was concerned they would wreck his weir to get at the herring.

"They got to be got rid of," he said. Karl could just see his wind-whipped red cheeks puffing out each word.

"He's right," said Karl's dad, as Karl flinched, "need to get 'em outta there before they ruin the fishing for us."

"But dad, they're stuck in the mud."

"Don't you tell me what's wrong. You and that flighty Nettie and her books, and that flip you dance around with. That Nettie's lucky to have a house and a job to go with it. What do they know about lobstering? Without the lobsters there'd be no school or fire department and police."

Karl snuck away. Quietly he turned the knob on the kitchen door and trod lightly down the steps off the porch onto the path. No one locked their doors in Quarry Cove and Pepper Mill. It was much easier getting in and out of the house. Same with the cars and trucks, everyone just left the keys in the ignition.

A big yellow moon dodged in and out of some gray clouds as he sauntered down to the bridge. By the big rock that overlooked the pool, he stopped. The police cruiser was parked by the railing, as though it hadn't moved. A tiny red dot of a cigarette glowed and dimmed from behind the wheel. He heard an occasional low, raspy metallic squawk over the police radio, and that was all that was left of the day's excitement.

Dodging from rock to fence, past empty trash cans, stacks of lobster traps and coils of rope, Karl scanned the pool for the whales.

Shaggy gray clouds briefly unveiled the moon, and it was in that one instance that he could readily make out two huge mounds, which had to be Bustah and Bumpah lying contentedly in the mud. All seemed quiet, except for the incoming tide licking the rocks.

He looked off down the estuary, past the lobster boats tethered to buoys, to the skiffs on both sides of the pool hitched to the floats. Farther down at the end of Mollusk Point, a light still shone through the curtains of the lighthouse keeper's home. Above it, the flashing light arched back and forth across The Narrows, where many a ship had perished before the light was built.

Nettie Beal wouldn't go to bed. Karl couldn't imagine Nettie sitting down reading a book, much less listening to the radio. In all likelihood, she would be pacing the brick tile floor of the kitchen, stopping at the window that overlooked Mollusk Point Causeway and the pool.

He looked back toward the whales. For a second, he thought he heard a croaking, muffled crackling sound, not as clear as the clickety-click sound the whales usually made.

A blanket of cold shuddered through his body as he struggled to adjust his eyes in the dim light. Could it be, he thought, could it be that they had died because they were out of the water? How would they survive unless they got back into the sea? Even when the tide rose, he asked himself, would they be able to pull themselves free of the mud?

He walked along the pool banks back onto the road, and slowly inched across the bridge, then down the bank to the rail. The whales were closer at this point than from the other side.

With the police cruiser not far away, he took a step, then stopped, anxiously listening for a telltale click or blow hole gasp of air. But there was nothing. He sat down in front of a small cedar bush staring across the pool at the two mounds. The whales both lay quietly on their bellies in the same spot they were earlier. Their snouts much like porpoises with a large bump of yellow whale fat for a hat.

The fingers that gently tightened on his shoulder tensed his whole body, as a smiling face came into view. A long finger covered her lips.

"Sssh," whispered Nettie Beal, squatting down beside him, "don't want to awaken our gendarmes, do we?"

"Hungry?"

She pushed a ham sandwich toward him, which he eagerly took and gobbled down.

"I guess you were," she said.

"What's going to happen? Will they die being out of the water so long?" Karl asked.

Nettie raised her finger, cautioning him. "If they can get out on this incoming tide, they won't be hurting."

"Oh, great," Karl said.

"But on the other hand, we've got to make sure that they get out. Right now, the lobstermen are shouting that they'll lose their catch and the police chief is worried about the traffic clogging the road."

"I heard him on the radio—and you, too."

"Meet the most hated person in Pepper Mill and Quarry Cove," she said, chuckling as she offered him her hand.

Karl shook it.

"If you're seen with me, you will be the second most hated person in town."

"I don't care. What a bunch of rotten people!"

"Now, now, don't forget that includes a lot of people, some who might feel the same way you and I do about the whales."

32

"I know. But my dad…and…that jerk Tripper Gleason…the seiners and weir keepers—they're all the same."

A car door quietly opened behind them, and they sat still.

"What's going on?" Joe Mullins said, looking down at the duo. "Kinda late to be sitting out here, ain't it?"

"We just thought we'd keep an eye on the whales," Nettie said, standing, brushing off her jeans. "What are you doing, Joe? Making sure they don't attack the towns?"

Mullins guffawed.

"Naw, just making sure some people don't get carried away and start shooting."

"That'd make a lot of people happy," she said.

"Now don't you get carried away, Nettie. You know we have to protect the fishermen and make sure people can use the roads without being held up from getting to work."

Nettie turned on him. "I have nothing against that. There're just too many people with trigger-happy fingers around here. Look what happened last year when Tripper Gleason shot that Peregrine Falcon. Where were you then?"

Mullins shook his head. "Had nothin' to do with that."

"Yet, you're out here in force serving a police chief who wants to kill these whales because they're holding up traffic?"

"It's my job. I just do as I'm told."

"Do as you're told?" Nettie Beal scoffed and shook her head, disgustedly.

"Come on Karl, let's go home. There's nothing we can do here. At least – not until morning."

With that they both climbed the embankment, leaving Patrolman Bill Mullins dazed and alone on the dark embankment.

9

The Big Pileup

News of two "gigantic" whales visiting tiny Quarry Cove crackled from the radio and spread rapidly. By noon Tuesday, the whale visit was a top attraction. Hundreds of people had parked their cars, pickups, vans, bikes and motorcycles along Route 1A.

Geysers of brown water shot skyward like fountains, as the crowd cheered and big Bumpah lead little Bustah through a series of aquatic acrobatics. They were mainly rolls and dives, accompanied by the usual hooting, trumpeting, and squeals— and an unforgettable clickety-clack-clack rattle before a plunge, delighting the crowd.

People on both sides of the pool kept jockeying for the best photo angles. Radio reporters with tape recorders over their shoulders and a mic in their hands bumped through the crowd, snatching a bit of a conversation here and there, and asking people how they liked the show. Newspaper reporters from Bangor, Portland, Bar Harbor, Belfast, Ellsworth, and Rockland surrounded an exasperated Harrington, while Officer Joe Mullins basked in the attention.

"This'll pull the tourists in," a truck driver gleefully yelled into a radio mike.

Chief Harrington shook his head when he heard that and tapped the driver on the elbow.

"That your rig—the one with the red cab?"

The driver raised his hand in acknowledgement.

"You'd better move it. This road is getting jammed."

Joe Mullins's arms were like a pinwheel, trying to keep the busy 1A traffic moving as reporters yelled questions to him in-between stopping traffic to allow an occasional pickup or car to cross the bridge.

"Sheriff says there's a deputy on the way," the chief shouted to Mullins, as a reporter held out a mic.

"About time, too. I've been on this job since yesterday and barely had time for a smoke."

"What's the next step, Chief?" WBCF-Radio announcer Malcolm Hadlock of Portland asked, his eyes eagerly awaiting a reply, as he pushed the mic into the chief's face.

"Can't say…"

"Are you planning to shoot the whales?" Hadlock said, with his deep, well-modulated Boston accent.

"I'm watching the situation very closely," the chief replied, elbowing his way down to the fence.

"It's been reported that you are…" Hadlock's voice trolled after him. The chief shook his palm, lowered his head, and strode down the embankment.

"Although he's been quoted as saying he would dispose of the whales unless they move back to sea, the chief would not comment about what he said yesterday. This is Malcolm Hadlock reporting for WBCF-Radio at the junction of Quarry Cove and Pepper Mill, home of the world famous Mollusk Point Lighthouse, and now the home of two gigantic Beluga whales, Bustah and Bumpah."

Chief Harrington looked like he'd been hit by a bait bucket. For a couple of seconds he just stared blankly as the two whales did a curtain call to the roar of the crowd, then he spun around and marched up to Malcolm Hadlock, who was excitedly recording a conversation with two children.

The chief stood stunned.

"We don't want the whales to get shot," a little boy said.

"Only nasty people would shoot a whale, especially Bustah and Bumpah," his sister said.

Malcolm Hadlock beamed and thanked the kids and their mother, who added, "It's horrible to think that the police are planning to shoot these two beautiful innocent whales."

"Thank you," a delighted Malcolm Hadlock said, as the furious police chief, his face scorching red, fumed.

"So, there you have it. Nobody wants to see these two delightful and wonderful whales harmed. No matter...adults or children. They all love Bustah and Bumpah. For WBCF Radio in Portland, this is Malcolm Hadlock."

"Can I have a word with you?" the chief asked, his palms pleadingly open. Is the mic off?" he asked in a shaky voice. Hadlock extended the mic toward the chief.

"Not on the radio...with you!" the chief said, his face an explosive red, as he waved the mic aside. Hadlock lowered the mic to his side.

"Where do you get this business about the whales having names?" the chief said, his words strained between his lips.

"Oh, it's everywhere...radio, newspapers...they all have it."

"What?" The chief appeared ready to explode, as Hadlock held the mic at waist height, eager to catch an outburst.

Briefly, the chief stared at Hadlock, who raised the mic again as the chief angrily shook his head, spun around and made a beeline toward Nettie Beal.

"You'd better watch it," he started, as Nettie turned toward him with a smile. "You've got everybody thinking these whales have names, and you know what that means, don't you?"

"So...what's wrong with that?"

"What?"

"Having a name? Where would we be without names? You certainly wouldn't like to be referred to as 'it' or 'that,' would you?"

"I could get you for inciting...well...a riot...," he said with a gulp.

"Where?" Nettie flung her forearm and flipped her palm. "I don't see any riot, Chief."

His face jelled tomato red with anger, the chief swung around and walked back up the embankment to the police cruiser, brushing aside reporters as he mumbled angrily under his breath.

10

The Rift Widens

"I can't wait to get out of here," Christine told Karl later as she sat across from him at the school cafeteria lunch table, "...can't wait."

"Me, too. Only hope Nettie is down there in case they try…"

"Try what? They'd better not!"

"But what can we do if they all show up with rifles?"

"I don't know, but Nettie will be working on a plan, that's for sure."

They'd barely closed their lunch boxes when Roger Millett, the school guidance counselor, appeared at the door and raised his hand.

"Assembly hall," he said.

They both sat in the front row waiting for Principal Brown who was busy talking with a cluster of teachers at the steps to the stage.

"I won't keep you long, I just want to let you know that we are having problems at the pool, and the police have asked that you keep your distance until they get rid—"

"Get rid?" Christine sprang to her feet, horrified.

"I mean…well, until they resolve the situation. Now please sit down."

Reluctantly, Christine sat down as Tripper Gleason mocked her.

"Please don't hurt my whale-ees…please…" he whined.

"That's enough. Quiet," Mr. Millet said, stepping onto the stage. "No more interruptions." His face was in an uncharacteristic blush.

Karl shook his fist at Gleason, who taunted him, barely audibly, "Come on."

Principal Brown urged caution.

"Be careful around the pool. These whales might be dangerous."

Christine scoffed. Brown stared hard at her.

"We don't know, so, you'd better be careful."

"But Miss Brown, they're Beluga whales, members of a very friendly species and—" she started.

"Well how do we know? Are you an expert on whales?"

Gleason guffawed and the assembly broke into laughter, and Mr. Millet climbed back onto the stage raising a finger to the crowd.

"Perhaps we could begin a study on whales. So why don't you kick it off and bring a paper in tomorrow Mr. Gleason, explaining what these whales are?"

There was dead silence. Miss Brown nodded that the assembly was dismissed and strode off the stage, her high heels clicking like a tack hammer.

A crowd swirled around Christine as she and Karl waited for the bus.

"You were great, Christine," someone shouted, and there was a roar of approval, as a cluster of students surrounded her.

"Don't let that bonehead Gleason bother you," six-foot Tiny Stinson yelled. "If he gives you any guff I'll take care of him. Where is he anyway?"

"Talking to Mr. Millett, he doesn't want to write that paper about whales," said Kathleen Rice, with the crowd pinning a tail of laughter on her comment.

Gleason dashed across the quad, the last student to board the bus. He scowled at Christine and Karl and slumped into a seat.

"Please, Mr. Millet, don't make me write about the whales," Tiny Stinson said.

Gleason twisted his head, about to say something when Stinson started to stand up. Gleason turned back, mumbling.

Christine nudged Karl, with a smile stretched across her face, her blue steel eyes sparkling.

The bus driver would normally cross Route 1A, drop Karl and let the Dickinson boys off at the bridge, then make a U-turn and go home. But that afternoon, Elwood Tinker came up against a solid wall of human flesh circling the police cruisers and pressed against the fence around the pool.

"Look at the crowd," Christine said, "looks like the whole state is here."

Together, she and Karl jumped down the steps and started toward the water. The State Police had cordoned off the bridge to Quarry Cove.

"Do you live up there?" a tall trooper asked Karl, then waved him through. Other troopers were directing traffic past the bridge as Officer Mullins and Chief Harrington directed the cars that were backing off the grass bank alongside the pool.

"Oh…look," Christine cried out, as Bumpah and Bustah treated the ever-swelling crowd to an early matinee.

Mighty slaps echoed across the cove as Bustah did a back flip with a trumpet, and crashed back into the pool. Bumpah rolled and flashed two racks of white pointed teeth, winked at the crowd with his tiny peephole eyes, and disappeared below the swirling water. The crowd yelled and ducked and laughed, as frothy white foam showered them.

Bustah half surfaced and shot a jet of brownish water out of the blowhole just behind the round melon-colored cone on top of his head.

"They look a lot like dolphins," Karl said, rubbing his hands excitedly as Bustah rolled again, did a flip, let out a toothy clickety-click and dove in again.

"I bet they know we're here," Christine said.

A trooper yelled to them from the end of the bridge, "You can't stand there. You'll have to move."

Halfway up Quarry Cove Hill they perched atop a large rock that overlooked the pool.

The banks on both sides of the pool were a mass of red jackets, blue sweaters, head scarves, picnic hampers and baby carriages filled with screeching babies. Kids shouted and waved. Horns blared from rigs, and cars tooted as they passed, drivers and passengers waving to the crowd.

But amid this gathering of humanity, one thing stood out sharp and clear on the opposite bank.

"Look. Down there next to that shrub," Karl excitedly pointed as he jumped around.

"It's Nettie," Christine said. "Just look at her."

Nettie stood just as firmly as she had on the first day when she confronted the police and the game wardens. Her strong hands, hardened by myriad rough jobs, braced a broom handle against her right shoulder.

Tacked above it on a piece of white cardboard in big, bold black letters, she had written, "SAVE THE WHALES."

"I've got to go – see you later." Christine rushed back across the bridge to Nettie, took the sign and waved it at Karl. He waved back and had started to run down the hill when his dad drew alongside him in his cut-down Pierce Arrow luxury car, now a pickup, piled high with traps and buoys.

"Get in. Never mind that foolishness," he said.

"I was going to join Christine."

"Forget it, and climb in. We're both late for supper. You know somebody's goin' to get hurt if they keep that mess up. You ain't part of it, I hope?"

"But dad – there's no problem, no mess – just a couple of whales struggling to get back to the ocean."

"They're up river feeding off the herring and clams, and every darned thing that we fish for," his dad said, angrily hitting the steering wheel as he turned into the little driveway of the white Cape.

"Anyway, we'll put a stop to it tonight," his dad said, angrily slamming the door and defiantly striding past Karl up the steps onto the front porch.

"Flounder?" Karl's eyes widened as his mother set the plate before him and offered him a dish of peas.

"I love flounder," he said, as his mother smiled and ladled out French fries.

"Then eat it. Be lucky if there's any left after those whales leave."

"Now, Earl," his mother cautioned. "There's a better way."

His dad shook his head disgustedly. "What've I done to deserve this? Bad enough having half the state yelling and screaming because they've never seen a whale before. Now, I've got a son who's fallen in love with 'em."

Shaking his head, he got up from the table, angrily pushing the chair back as his wife stood quietly by.

"Where are you going?"

"To the meetin'," he said, pulling his rolled down hip boots on. "It'll put an end to this mess, or I'll eat my hat."

11

Breaking the Bond

The First Congregational Church buzzed with excitement as Pepper Mill and Quarry Cove folks struggled to get a seat in the pews. The selectmen's office at Pepper Mill could never hold more than twenty people.

Radio and newspaper reporters bounced among the crowd, grabbing comments here and there from those anxious to be heard on radio, or better yet, to get a picture in the newspapers. But there were few takers. Despite the gravity of the situation, most, if not all of the people were very reserved, steeped in old fashioned Yankee conservatism.

Christine yelled to Karl as she raced up the street from her father's pickup.

"They were going to keep it a secret," she said excitedly. "But they failed."

She held up a cardboard sign worded with bold black letters: "DON'T KILL THE WHALES!"

"I made you one, too," she said, peeling another piece of cardboard from her sign: "STOP THE WHALE KILLERS!"

"Now, all you have to do is wait for Nettie's signal. When she stands up, we stand up and hold our cards above our heads, and boo."

"Boo, jeer, yell, if you have to. But drown them out."

Together they edged through a crowd of retired lobstermen with their wives and children, until they managed to wedge themselves into a pew, about three rows behind his parents who stared solemnly ahead.

Chief Harrington, in a starched white shirt with a black Sam Brown belt running across his chest to his gun belt, made a dignified stride to the podium that stood before the cloth-covered altar just in front of the church's stained glass windows. Solemnly, he raised his hand as fishermen cheered and whistled.

"Glad you could all make it. It's a tight fit, but with luck on our side, we should be out by midnight." Laughter and whistles echoed through the church, and the chief beamed in appreciation.

"Now, now," he said, an appreciative grin sweeping his face, as he introduced Pepper Ridge and Quarry Cove First Selectman, and the moderator who, somewhat reluctantly, stepped up to the podium.

"We have a problem," Chauncey Philpot of Pepper Mill started, and the crowd laughed and shouted support.

"An' don't ya think we know it," a voice shouted.

"Yeah, we didn't come for no baked bean supper," rang out another, as the crowd cheered and stomped their feet on the wooden floor.

Philpot's narrow shy face reddened. He forced a smile. Facing an angry crowd was not in his portfolio. He'd worked at Pepper Mill Savings & Loan for most of his sixty years. It was an experience that had turned him into a reclusive and shy individual. With light blond hair and a balding scalp, a large pair of brown bifocal glasses rested uncomfortably on his short narrow nose.

"Ladies and gentlemen," he tried again, as the fishermen mumbled and groaned. Philpot winced and bit his lower lip.

"If you don't have courtesy to hear this man, why don't you leave?"

The church went quiet except for the clang as someone knocked over a folding chair. All heads turned to the center of the church.

Nettie Beal stood grim and defiant, with both hands on her hips, as her eyes slowly swept the crowd.

"Go ahead," she said, and sat down.

"We have a – what I want to tell you is we will do everything, that is we – Pepper Mill and Quarry Cove – will do everything we can to resolve this crisis."

"Crisis?" Nettie's voice rose with her. "Mr. Mayor, or Mr. First Selectman, whatever it is, please don't be misled by these fishermen that this is a crisis."

Karl's dad was on his feet. Face flushed, stern and glazed, his right stubby index finger pointed at Nettie.

"I've had enough of this and you, Nettie Beal. Enough's enough. You're responsible for stirring up these people." His hand swept the audience. "Yeah, and even the kids in the villages, including my own."

Defiantly, Nettie held up her sign. Christine sprang to her feet, her sign above her head. Karl jumped up too. His father glared at him.

Most of the fishermen angrily rose to their feet as more kids held signs above their heads as they stood and started to chant.

"Save the whales…Save the whales..."

Chief Harrington walked up behind Philpot and raised both hands trying to get the sign wavers to sit down. But the chanting continued, and signs continued to be waved back and forth.

"S-a-v-e… T-h-e… W-h-a-l-e-s. S-a…"

Shaking his head in disbelief, Woody Harrington looked hopelessly at the selectmen seated behind him, who lowered their heads in embarrassment.

"You know," he started, as the noise continued. The fishermen were shouting at the sign wavers who continued to chant. "Something's got to be done, and something will be done."

"Well then, get on with it," Karl's father shouted, as the crowd settled down a bit. "If you can't do anything, we will."

"Now, I got to warn you Seth an' you want to hear me loud an' clear – if there's any disturbing of the peace—"

"Disturbing the peace?"

45

"That's right. If you take matters into your own hands, I hate to tell ya but I'll have to arrest ya."

The crowd went quiet, except for the stuttering whirr of WBCF-TV's 16-millimeter camera.

"Now ain't that a nice kettle of fish. I've come here to find out what the towns are going to do and I get threatened to be put in jail." Seth Bunker said, despairingly holding his hands up.

"You can't just go out and shoot those whales." Heads switched to the left side of the church when a short man in checkered shirt and his rolled down fishing boots stood up. Karl looked surprised at Christine. Her jaw dropped.

"Dad?" a surprised half whisper escaped her lips. Even more surprised, her face mushroomed into a giant smile.

Ronald Alley's weather-beaten face broke into a smile as he faced Karl's dad. Leaning on the pew in front of him, he waited for a reply from an angry Seth.

"Oh, so now we've got the dealers going after us…"

"I've got just as much to lose as you have, Seth…dealer or no dealer. I just think there's a better solution to this than just picking up a gun and shooting a couple of whales who strayed into our pool."

"Our pool? Oh, now it's our pool? Did you hear that? Here's a man who lives in Pepper Mill – mile from the pool, and he's callin' it 'our pool'?"

A rumble of support lifted from some of the lobstermen's ranks. "Yea," as their heavy rubber boots shuffled uneasily between the church pews.

"It's just as much our pool as it is yours," Ronald Alley shouted back, bringing a crowd of supporters to their feet with a chorus of, "Yea."

"Thank you, Mr. Alley. Thank you," Nettie said, as she thrust the sign above her head. "Thank you." Her upraised palm brought a crowd of students to their feet, all cheering and waving signs.

Christine sprang to her feet.

"Yea...alright dad!" she called out as she flag-waved her sign. She lowered the sign, shocked as she caught sight of Karl hastily scrambling through the crowd and out the front door of the church.

Chief Harrington rested both hands on the podium and shook his head with disgust as kids and some grown-ups reached for Ronald Alley's hand, patting and thumping his shoulders with excitement.

"That's all we need. That's all I need...that's for sure," Chief Harrington told a dazed Joe Mullins. "Now we've got Quarry Cove and Pepper Mill split, split right down the ruddy middle...this could mean... now the fish an' chowdah's going to fly."

"What d'you mean, Chief?"

Harrington just shook his head. "All I know is that we have one of the worst traffic problems this state...yeah, this state...has ever seen, and something's got to be done...an' fast. B'sides we don't want no wars...neither."

"Does that mean, I mean, what will happen to the cruiser?"

"We'll have to cut it in half," a disgusted chief scoffed. Mullins looked dazed.

First Selectman Chauncey Philpot cautiously rose from his seat and walked timidly up to the pulpit. He waited, as the chief sat down.

Raising his right hand to bring order, the crowd shuffled back into their seats and Chauncey, obviously feeling some restored confidence, waved his palm at the audience.

"If there's no further business to come before this board," he said with a swallow, and a cough, "then I'll call for a motion to adjourn."

Another selectman behind him shouted a second to the motion. Chauncey quickly tapped the podium with his gavel and with a thin voice declared, "Meeting adjourned."

"You'd better stick around, Joe," the chief said, grabbing Joe Mullins's forearm. Mullins's eyes widened. "There could be trouble," the chief said, his face taut.

"I ain't had much sleep since this whole thing happened, chief," Mullins said, shaking his head.

"Get down to the pool and make sure nobody's standing around with guns. If they are, send 'em home…or—"

"What?"

"Arrest them. We ain't goin' to have no shooting around here…not as long as I'm chief."

Mullins nodded his head as he helped his wife to her feet. "Joe ain't had much sleep since these blessed whales came up the pool, Buddy. Can't ya get some relief for him?"

"He'll be alright, Clara. I'll relieve him as soon as I can," the Chief said. "B'sides, I got a state trooper coming down from Orono to help out."

Turning to leave, the Chief paused, and walked back to Joe.

"Another thing, Joe…"

Joe stiffened, waiting for the worst.

"If that Nettie Beal is down there waving that frig…sorry, Clara…sign, then arrest her."

Joe's mouth dropped open.

Squaring the rimmed cap on his head, Chief Harrington turned on his heels and strode to the front door of the church, his fingers drumming his black leather holster.

WBCF's News at Eleven had caught all the action, especially the exchange between Seth Bunker, Karl's dad, and Ronald Alley, Christine's dad.

"Tonight's meeting surprised everyone. Up to now, these two communities have shared just about everything—schools, fire department, and police. But tonight's meeting may result in an irreparable split. Most folk around here feel that it will take some time before citizens recover from this night of disagreement."

48

Karl grimaced as he watched the television reporter, while pressing himself into the chair as his father bristled, and leaned across the kitchen table staring hard at the small black and white TV.

"We can solve this without everyone going off the deep end," Christine's dad said into the camera.

"Do you believe that this will cause a split in the communities?" Mathew Hadlock breathlessly asked.

"I shouldn't think so, do you?" Christine's dad shot back into the camera. "I just think we all have to exercise a little tolerance and not overreact."

Hadlock's concerned voice excitedly injected, "Here's what Seth Bunker of Quarry Cove had to say…" as he extended the mic toward Seth Bunker.

Staring angrily into the camera, Seth shouted, "We'll have those fr… whales outta that pool b'fore much longer." Karl swallowed hard as he recalled his dad angrily pushing past people in the church aisle and waving a fist disgustedly at Nettie, who grinned, waved back, and blew him a kiss.

"What will this do for the communities?" Hadlock shouted after Karl's dad.

"Who cares? I sure as h… eh, heck don't."

"But aren't some of these people your friends?"

"I don't call 'em that anymore, not when they turn on their neighbors like this," Karl's dad shouted back at Blaine, and the picture faded and switched to Upjohn's Used Cars of Portland commercial.

Seth Bunker clicked off the TV, leaned back in his chair, grunted and pounded the kitchen table. "There – that'll fix 'em."

"You should be ashamed of yourself," Karl's mom said to her husband. "That's disgusting to act like that. Whatever will they think of us around here?"

"I don't give a rat's… eh, rat's tail. They ain't friends o' mine that'll let you down like that."

"I'm going home to bed," Karl said, as he stood up.

"I ain't through by a long shot. You wait and see. It's all that durned Nettie Beal's fault. But she'll get hers – just ya wait an' see."

"Now what has Nettie done to get ya so mad?" Karl's mom said.

Karl, shoulders hunched, walked out of the kitchen.

"You've got him all upset," his mom said.

"He'll be even more upset, when we get through with Nettie."

Karl stopped outside the kitchen door and listened.

"She's had a nice run of it, she has…free house and good pay. Well, we'll see what her boss says when he hears about this mess."

"Seth, whadya mean?" his mother asked. "Nettie has worked hard at that job and don't you think the Coast Guard doesn't know it," she said, slapping the dishcloth over the sink.

Karl pressed his head against the door frame, not wanting to miss a word.

"The Coast Guard ain't goin' to let her get away with what she's doin' – that's for sure. They'll kick her out…you wait an' see…you'll see."

"And all of this, just because she loves the whales? How ridiculous. Ooh, you do come up with strange things."

Karl angrily stomped upstairs, as the kitchen door opened and his mother called out to him. His father sat on the sofa, his face in a scowl, staring at the TV as a quartet joyfully harmonized a ditty about the thrill of using the smoothest shaving cream. Karl looked down the stairs amazed, as his father hummed along with the ditty, "…the smoothest, freshest and kissingest face in all the world…wow!"

His mother raised her hand, shook her head, smiled, and bid him goodnight.

Karl sat on the edge of his bed staring out the window that overlooked the pool at the bottom of the hill. Here and there, little dabs of light flickered as traffic slowly worked its way up and down 1A.

Except for the bouncy commercial jingles and growling voices of the TV show downstairs and some squeaky doors, he couldn't hear any other sounds, and nothing coming from the pool.

Looking out into the night, Karl felt desolate. It was unfathomable to even think that this situation and this conflict would ever arise between two tiny fishing communities. Now it seemed they were split apart, lobstermen against dealers, and even families against each other. But, even worse than that, what would happen now to Christine and him? How could he ever explain to her why he left? He was scared, scared of his father. And now he sat furious with himself.

He was still tearing apart his conscience when the door opened and his father stepped across the threshold. His face was somber and he looked as mean as the day he found two of his trap lines cut.

"I want ya to keep yer distance from that Nettie…and that Alley girl," he snapped, and closed the door behind him.

"But, Dad—"

An hour or so later, he could hear his dad and mom talking as they lay in bed. His dad's deep sleepy voice growled as his mother chuckled, taunting him, and making him even angrier.

A warm lavender-scented breeze rustled from a huge bush just below his window, its seductive fragrance floating invisibly and contentedly into his room. It reminded him of Christine. Now, except for an occasional tiny tap of the shade's cord against the sill, Quarry Cove was finally going to sleep.

The shade tapping the sill was so peaceful; it was as though he was aboard the *Clamshell*, his fourteen-foot dinghy. Slowly his body reached out for sleep, sinking him into a reflective warm southerly breeze just off Islesboro. As the mainsail curved and stiffened, the yellow telltales straightened, and he came about heading back into the cove. The creak and ping of the boom in the Gooseneck drew him deeper into sleep, as the lick of water against the prow suddenly gave way to a swish and a snapping sound. It was like someone drawing a stick across fence palings.

Clickety-click-clack.

Karl sat bolt upright. Quickly, he slipped into his wind breaker and tiptoed out of the house down to the rock.

Ghostly shapes of trees, bushes, and lobster traps stepped out of the darkness as his eyes focused. His ears were on alert for telltale sounds that would indicate Bustah and Bumpah were still in the pool. But for a zephyr metallically rustling the leaves of a birch, and the faint bass hoot of an owl, it was quiet.

A quick sprint took him to the bridge. Both sides of the pool were deserted, except for the faint glitter of chrome of the police car's fender between the railings on the opposite side of the pool.

Halfway across the bridge he leaned over the rail searching for a trace of the whales. Except for a wash of waves on rocks and the muffled and hollow rub of dinghies and punts nestling up against the floats, all was unusually quiet.

"They're gone."

He jumped as a huge shadow formed the shape of Joe Mullins.

"Jumpy, eh?" he said with a laugh, leaning on the rail alongside Karl.

"You mean they're no longer here?"

"That's right. Left on the high tide, thank the Lord, an' I hope they don't come back."

Karl lowered his head. "That's too bad. I wanted to see them again."

"Too bad? My gawd, boy, don't ya realize the troubles they caused around here? It's already created a split between Quarry Cove and Pepper Mill. Chief's already sweatin' over what's goin' to happen if the towns split – and what'll happen to the police department. We share the cruiser, you know?"

"But, why?" Karl asked, looking into Mullins' tense face.

"It's the fishing, ooh, and the traffic. Chief's really upset over that."

"Oh, I know all about that," Karl interrupted him. "Dad's so mad that I can't see Christine anymore, all because her dad stood up at the meeting tonight."

"Oh, it'll be even worse than that – much worse."

"Whadya mean? You make it sound like it's nothing. Christine and I have been friends since we started school – what could be worse than being told to stay away from your best friend?"

Joe Mullins drummed his fingers on the rail, slowly shaking his head in understanding.

"Oh, I know, dads can be hard at times."

"So what else can happen?" Karl asked, looking anxiously at Mullins. "What could be worse than that?"

Mullins lit up a cigarette, and dragged deeply as his words floated out on a smoke cloud.

"People around here don't get up in arms unless they're really upset. I mean, well, look at how Nettie carried on, ya know, on the shore here, and at the meeting. That was no way for a woman – a lady– to act, especially after what the towns did for her after she lost Phil."

"But she's always run the light good…nobody ever went aground," Karl said, looking hard at Mullins. "Whadya mean?"

Mullins took a long drag on his cigarette. His eyes narrowed with a deep furrow across his brow as the smoke streamed out of his nostrils. Karl struggled to hold back a laugh. It was as though Cowpoke Mullins was readying for a reckoning at the OK Corral.

"If it hadn't bin for – well, for yer dad, for one, and the most of the villagers – she wouldn't be living where she is." He paused, taking on a proud posture as he stared at Karl.

"She got a good deal. They were able to convince the Coast Guard to let her stay in the house rent-free, just as long as she took care of the light, ya know – make sure the generator was running and the light was working."

"So, she's working," Karl started. "She's paying her rent by caring for the light."

Mullins nodded and twisted his head to one side, apparently not sure he wanted to say anymore.

A strange feeling started to rise in Karl's stomach. He looked and waited for Mullins to continue. But the officer turned and started to walk off the bridge.

"So what's going to happen to Nettie?" Karl said reaching for the officer's forearm.

"Didn't say anything was…just thinking of what the people did for her, and what would happen if they all decided they didn't like what she was doing."

Mullins raised his hand in a farewell salute.

"Wait! You mean to tell me that these people would kick her out?"

Mullins kept walking.

"Gotta go, Karl. Take care, I got to call the chief an' tell him the good news."

Karl was just two steps from stepping off the bridge when he heard it again.

Clicker-click-clack.

Stopping dead in his tracks, Karl slowly turned his head. The Pepper Mill & Quarry Cove cruiser dipped in a gravel washout as Mullins pulled out of the parking lot. Losing no time, Karl ran back to the center of the bridge and stared hard into the water. Waves gently licked the rocks, but it was hard to see much except a dark carpet of water flecked with foam.

Suddenly, a white bubble of foam fanned out on the surface, followed by a pop as the bubble burst, followed by a trail of smaller bubbles.

Bustah and Bumpah were playing it cozy, nestled together and snoring away at the bottom of Quarry Cove.

Happy the whales were still there, but angered at what Joe Mullins told him, Karl's sneakers ground into the gravel as he marched back up Quarry Cove Road. Even as he trailed the gravel across the kitchen linoleum, anger and fear wrestled for control of his mind. He was angry at his dad and the others... especially Joe Mullins and the Chief. But even more fearful that the cowardice he displayed at the meeting would mean he would lose Christine.

12

Face Off

Sleep was a series of head drops and jerky awakenings. Karl barely slept, and shot out of the house the next morning, right by his dad who was pulling on his thick, long, woolen, gray socks with the red ring around the tops.

Christine was climbing out of her dad's truck as he ran across the bridge. For a second, she just stared at him, then turned around and walked slowly along the railing where a gang of kids were feverishly chatting and searching for Bustah and Bumpah.

"They must have gone," he said, as Christine turned, a cold angry look across her face.

"What happened? Your dad shoot them?"

"That's a heck of a thing to say. They must have gone on the ebb tide last night," he said walking after her as she strutted away.

"What's up?"

"Plenty. What's up with you? The way you left the meeting last night was as if we were all through because my dad took on your dad."

He struggled for some explanation and fumbled so much, Christine just stared at him.

"You were scared, weren't you? You didn't want your dad to see me with you?"

"I'm sorry." He searched her face for forgiveness. Could that cold look dissolve into a warm radiant look? "I was muddled up."

She stood there in front of the cedar bush that had almost been crushed by the crowds the day before.

"I'm sorry. It won't happen again. "Believe me…it won't."

"Promise?"

He nodded, and she gave him a peck on his cheek. Some of the kids behind them made a whoop and she kissed him again. His face flushed into a crimson glow.

He couldn't wait to tell her about his talk with Mullins, as she shuffled and shook her shoulders irritably in the bus seat beside him.

"It just doesn't make sense," she said, still upset from what he'd done. "I can't believe your father was so mean."

"Oh, he'll get over it," he said. She just shook her head.

"Anyway, as far as I'm concerned, I'm not paying attention to him," he said, tightening his chin and staring determinedly at her.

She swung around. "What did he say about you and me? Does he hate me as much as Nettie?"

"He's upset. He's pretty mad...so mad, he's even..."

"Go on. Soon he'll be saying he doesn't want you to see me—if he hasn't already." She twisted in her seat staring directly into his crimson face.

"Knew it," she said, as Karl swallowed hard. "Well?"

"He said he thought it would be best if we didn't see each other. But...even worse..." She stood up, squeezed past him and settled in a seat next to a surprised and happy Billy Smith.

"Ooh, Karl," a girl behind him giggled.

"Poor baby," Tripper Gleason tittered, as the others chuckled.

He sprang out of his seat, swung on a surprised Gleason two seats back, and sent a right and a left into his face. Gleason twisted and dodged the fury of Karl's blows as the bus ground to a stop.

"You... Off!" the bus driver shouted, his long index finger pointing the path to the door.

"I'll get ya back for that," Gleason yelled after him.

Karl shook his head and hopped down the steps.

A shocked Christine stared at him as the bus pulled away and he just glared back. It wouldn't have happened if she hadn't moved, he thought, taking a kick at a small rock.

He covered the remaining quarter of a mile to school on a dog trot. Students were shuffling through the main glass doors from the recess area as he strode boldly through the gates.

The bus swung around and pulled over as the driver opened the door.

"What got into ya?" he said, shaking his head in disbelief. "Never seen ya act like that before. Shoulda waited until you was off the bus."

"He's a pain in the butt," Karl replied, as the driver smiled and nodded his head in agreement.

"He's the big shot football player. I'd watch out for him from now on. He's a pretty big guy, ya know," the driver said, as Karl nervously watched the end of the line of students enter the building.

"I gotta run," he said, as the driver gave him a thumbs-up and the line got even shorter. And there, straining to see over the heads of the students was Christine. But when he caught her eye, she quickly turned her head.

"Hey, Karl," the bus driver called, his head straining down the steps of the bus. "Don't worry – I didn't report ya." Karl waved a thanks and ran off as the driver tooted his horn.

Mr. Millett was standing on stage in the auditorium all sharpened up in his black pin-striped suit. Karl plunked himself into a front row seat. Christine was seated three rows back, and looked at him somewhat puzzled – and, he thought, a little worried.

"I am here to report that the whales that paid us a friendly visit have now departed," Millett said, as the students murmured incoherently, except for Tripper Gleason.

"Thank gawd for that," he said.

Millett stopped abruptly and stared hard at Gleason.

"Ah, yes, as I remember," Millett said, walking off the stage towards Gleason, "you were going to surprise us all this morning with your dissertation on whales," he said. He raised his eyebrows and his cheeks pinched into a smile.

Gleason cleared his throat as his buddies tittered and stared at him. The girls chuckled.

"Well, Mr. Gleason?"

"I have something," he mumbled, barely audible.

"Wonderful. I knew you'd come through. Come on...onto the stage and give us the benefit of your knowledge of the Delphinapterus leucas," he said.

Gleason gulped.

"What?"

Millett lowered his head, deflecting a smile as the students chuckled, waiting expectantly as Gleason pulled a sheet of yellow legal paper out of his backpack.

The crowd sniffled, chuckled, and waited. Gleason scowled at some of them, bringing a temporary hush, before glaring at Karl who shook his fist at him.

"A whale is one big son of a gun," Gleason stumbled, bringing laughter from the assembly. He started to laugh too. "Well, they are," he emphasized, looking upset.

Millett quieted the group.

"Go on Mr. Gleason, that's an interesting opening statement."

The assembly laughed louder.

"He has a blow pipe on his head which squirts water..."

Students roared. Millett swallowed, suppressing a laugh, waving his hand trying to calm the assembly down, and encouraged Gleason to continue.

"Whales are fat. Their bellies are filled with blubber," Gleason struggled, as the assembly roared.

Principal Brown ran up the steps.

"Alright, alright, that's enough. Now you can either be quiet and allow Ryan to finish his presentation, or you can all entertain us tomorrow with your own versions," she said.

Nodding toward Gleason, she smiled and beckoned for him to continue.

"Whales can kill people," he began with renewed confidence, accompanied by a serious stare in Karl's direction. "Captain Ahab was murdered by a whale," he said with a grin, as a hush fell in the auditorium before the students broke out in uproarious laughter. Tripper Gleason's face went blank.

"That's all I have," he said, looking dejected.

"You did a good job," Principal Brown told him. "How about a nice round of applause for Ryan?"

A few palms slapped in the hall. Some students snickered, others snorted and others contemptuously murmured, "Teacher's pet."

Gleason walked by Karl to get his backpack.

"I'll get even with you," he said.

Christine walked up to Karl and stopped, her eyes searching for something in his face. Her lips moved as if to say something, but she turned and followed the other students down the hall to class.

Gleason didn't allow much time for Karl to finish his lunch before he strutted menacingly across the quad, where Karl was leaning against the ballpark fence. With shoulders hunched in as though he were about to tackle a quarterback, he lunged at Karl who swiftly sidestepped him and belted him across his ear.

Angrily, Gleason staggered back, and then with fists flailing, hammered away at Karl, who fell to the asphalt with a blow behind his neck.

Half dazed, he struggled to his feet, but Gleason lunged at him, battering him back to ground.

"Stay down," someone shouted. But Karl, somewhat dazed, managed to stand up and go into a defensive boxing stance. Both his eyes stung, and his lips tasted blood. Gleason, he thought, was out to flatten him. Groggily, he waited for the next assault from this six-foot tall, two-hundred-pound football champ.

He was still dizzily weaving, his fists jerking back and forth, when Tripper Gleason floated toward him like a huge balloon.

Rubbing his eyes clear of the stinging sweat, he braced himself as Ryan Gleason's shocked face stared down from the shoulders of Elwood "Tiny" Stinson's head. Gleason didn't say anything. He just hung on as Tiny spun him in an airplane spin just like they do TV wrestling.

A crowd was cheering Tiny on as Mr. Millett strode across the quad, and Tiny set a dizzy-looking Tripper Gleason up against the fence.

"What's going on, now?" Millet asked, as he drew abreast of Tiny.

"Just showin' Tripper the airplane spin – said he'd never seen it," Tiny said as his lips stretched into a wide smile.

She was standing across the quad. Standing there by herself, she looked hopelessly lost.

Karl waited, sniffing, wiping blood from his nose, blinking and rubbing his eyes.

Then she was beside him, clinging to his arm, staring into his face and dabbing the blood away with a hanky. He forced a smile, and she smiled back. Then she did something that only she knew how to do so well. Gently holding his face between her cool palms, she tenderly kissed his swollen lips. Karl fell back against the fence and almost passed out.

13

Nettie Stands Tall

After school, they wasted no time mounting their bikes and meeting up with each other at the foot of Quarry Cove Hill. Christine became nearly hysterical when Karl told her about his father's threat that Nettie could lose her house.

Fast and furiously, they pedaled from the cove along the narrow causeway, keeping abreast of the Pepper Mill & Quarry Cove police cruiser heading south on the opposite side of Route 1A.

"Look," Christine said, with a quick glance at the cruiser and her head bent over the handlebars. "Son of a gun…is he following us?"

"Looks like it…is it the Chief?"

"Can't tell," Karl said, as he skidded to a halt.

Christine swished her rear wheel alongside his, just outside the post office. The cruiser stopped briefly, and then turned around.

"Oh, no," Christine said. "Look. It's your dad."

She pointed to Seth Bunker's thirty-foot lobster boat rounding Mollusk Point as it headed to the pool. Tagging behind were three more boats leaving white wakes as their engines roared, hurrying to port.

Karl stared. His father shot him a hard look, and cut the throttle as he prepared to tie up at his mooring.

Christine raised her eyebrows.

"Boy, I know someone who's going to catch it."

"So what. I don't care."

The white clouds in the sky had rapidly changed to gray, and were now turning black. Thunder rumbled behind the Camden hills beyond Islesboro. A few remaining lobster boats were heading home.

Nettie waved to them from the porch as they rode up.

"You'd better come in," she said.

Inside, they sat and waited as a rumble of distant thunder shimmied across the water, bouncing around the hills and rocks. Jagged forks of lightning stabbed through the clouds.

Before entering the post office, Christine told Karl that unless Nettie brought it up about the threats to her job and home, then they would have to.

Around the kitchen table, they hungrily munched into Italian rolls filled with tomatoes, onions, salami and ham as Nettie turned on the lights and checked the seaside window to make sure the lighthouse beam was on.

"Well, that's good, everything's working. Been having a spot of trouble with that daylight switch, and they're going to fix it…sometime. Like everything else, it's always 'As soon I can.' But the good news is that Bustah and Bumpah are safe—at least for now. Quarry Cove is quiet and peaceful…the way folks around here like it."

Nettie's eyes widened as she waited, sitting at the table with a sandwich between her fingers.

"Well?" she said, with a smile puckering her lips.

"It's not good news, Nettie. Is it Karl?"

"What? About them trying to kick me out of this house?"

"You know, then?" Christine said surprised, grabbing Karl's arm.

"So let them try it. They'll have a fight on their hands if they do," Nettie said, just as a clap of thunder shook Christine and Karl, and a crack of lightning splintered across the window facing the lighthouse.

"Just goes to show," she said, seemingly unmindful of the weather and the news.

"Like these sandwiches? Got them at Johnny's, just before the whales left and he packed up and went back to Searsport. He did a good business this year with his sandwiches, dogs and burgers. And he got a head start on the Bangor fair this year, thanks to Bustah and Bumpah."

Christine and Karl just sat looking at her, somewhat puzzled. Nettie was not in the least bit worried, Karl thought. But then again, this could be her way of brushing away troubles as if they weren't even there.

Thunder and lightning rumbled and clashed like a steel drum band gone mad. Stilettos of lightning stabbed through the windows and bounced like sparks across the red-tiled kitchen floor.

"Getting a bit nasty, I'd say, like the folks hereabouts. Better cover your sandwiches, unless you want them toasted," she said, nodding toward a window pane that flashed with lightning. Nettie placed her sandwich to one side and walked slowly over to the window facing the lighthouse.

"If I've done so much wrong that those people want to take my home away from me, then let them," she said, staring through the window unperturbed by the storm. "If they can," she added determinedly, a big smile glowing on her face.

"Getting some breakers now," she said, spinning around. "Want to watch them from the lighthouse?"

They followed Nettie as she walked briskly through the covered walkway that linked the keeper's home to the lighthouse. Thunder and lightning boomed and crackled along the wooden corridor.

Inside the lighthouse, they weaved up the black iron spiral staircase, pausing to look through a narrow hatch, as Nettie called it. Just before they reached the dome where the light revolved slowly and gears whirred contentedly, they paused, out of breath, and leaned against another hatch.

A strong wind howled as they pushed open the hatch and stepped out onto the walkway.

Ten- or fifteen-foot foaming waves rolled toward the lighthouse splattering across the rocky cliff below.

"Fun, eh? Phil and I used to come up here when the storms were raging. He got some great shots. One of them even got on a calendar, and another got in that magazine that just got started—"

"Maine Coast," said Christine.

Nettie snapped her fingers.

"Karl's trying to sell some pictures he took, and I'm painting seascapes. We'll bring out our work next time."

"If I'm still here," Nettie said breaking into a grin.

An hour spun away as if in a minute as the trio greeted each explosive crash of a wave with wild laughs and shouts. The three were like white sheeted ghosts in the sweep of the light, startled by the continuous crash of lighting and the booming thunder.

Settled back in the kitchen around the table, the storm passed. The weather forecaster on the tiny television was drawing circles and arrows on a chalkboard as he explained the path of the storm. The black and white picture was streaked with lines, grayed out, jumping and bouncing with static.

"Ours is just the same," Karl said. "The picture isn't that good, is it?"

"Ours comes in pretty good, considering, ya know, distance and hills," Christine said.

"Phil used to get a kick out of this weatherman," Nettie said. "He chalks all over the board and by the time he's through, you can't see anything, and you don't know anything more about the weather than you did before he started. Phil used to blast him. 'Look out the window,' he'd say. 'Who needs a weatherman?'"

They finished their sandwiches, and Christine and Karl were both anxious to hear what Nettie would say about what the next step would be. But she skirted the subject.

"I'm going to be alright," she told them as they stood on the porch preparing to leave. The downpour had turned to a drizzle, and even though the sea continued to pound the cliffs, a three-quarter moon was trying to edge the clouds aside.

Halfway back to Quarry Cove, Christine pulled up. "What are you going to say when your dad sees you?" she asked.

"I don't know. Not yet anyway."

"But, what if he sees us together?"

Karl shrugged his shoulders. He'll just have to do what he has to do, I guess."

Christine waited hopefully for Karl to say more.

"I'm not splitting with you, that's for sure, just because you tried to save the whales," he said.

Christine smiled. He wished she had kissed him as they pedaled down to the bridge. Once there, she pulled up alongside him and granted his wish on his waiting lips.

She turned to ride home. "I like you, Karl," she said, her face beaming, as she waited.

"I...like...you...too..." he stumbled. Christine laughed and rode off. He stood leaning back against the bike seat. Halfway across the bridge she turned and waved again. She had to be the most beautiful girl he'd even seen, he thought. Her long brown hair waved behind her as she pedaled leisurely home toward Pepper Mill. When she came to Cook's Corner, she stopped and stared at him, her head cocked to one side, obviously wondering why he was still there.

This time, he waved, and she waved back. Then with both hands against her lips she blew him a gigantic kiss. An indescribable feeling swept his body and he recognized it as love. He had never felt like this around any other girl. So, this had to be – like it was in the movies, he thought – true, honest love. It had to be.

14

Man to Man

His dad was mad, but not as mad as Karl thought he would have been. Now the whales had left and he was happy about that—but not about seeing Karl with Ronald Alley's daughter.

"Just let's sit down and enjoy our supper," his mother said, trying to smooth out the situation, squeezing her husband's shoulders as he settled into his chair at the table.

They ate a New England boiled dinner in near silence, with his father occasionally looking at Karl, who dug into his corned beef, carrots and potatoes with relish, and thanked his mother for a delicious dish.

His father had a rugged fisherman's face. Battered by salt spray, whipped by icy winds and searing cold and cracked by the hot suns of summer, his skin was hardened like brown tanned leather.

He also had a good, rich smile that showed off all of his teeth and the furrowed lines in his forehead, but Karl knew that his dad's smile wasn't about to surface.

So, he plunged head first into it.

"What about Nettie's home?" he blurted out, as his father almost swallowed a potato.

There was a deafeningly empty silence as his father stared at his son's expectant face. His mother knotted her fists and tightened her face as she scowled at Karl.

Seth Bunker stared, mouth partially ajar, his hands gripping his knife and fork planted firmly on each side of his half-finished dinner plate.

"Well?" Karl asked again.

"What about her?" His dad scowled at him. "She's a blessed nuisance with her signs and all those kids screaming."

"Look. Everything's going to be alright," his mother said. "The whales have gone, so nothing's going to happen to Nettie—is there Seth?"

With his teeth mashing into his corned beef, Seth Bunker slowly rose out of his chair. "She's going to have to show some respect around here, if she wants to stay," he said, staring hard at Karl.

"That's not fair," Karl said, not knowing what was moving him to say it.

His father almost exploded.

"Fair? Do ya think it's fair when we all worked to let her stay in that house after Phil died, and now she's out shooting us down just because we want to move the whales?"

"She's not fighting you. She just doesn't want to see the whales harmed," Karl said. "I don't blame her. There's a better way. Or, at least there was when they were here."

His father leaned across the table as his mother looked on, exasperated. He angrily pointed his big forefinger, the one that carried the deep black scar at the top of the nail from when he'd sliced it with a bait knife.

"Let her continue and she'll be sorry she ever heard of Quarry Cove."

"You mean, Dad, you're prepared to get her kicked out of her home because she likes whales? Is that what you're saying?" Karl was up, backing out of the kitchen.

"It's not that. It's how she puts them before us fishermen, and—another thing. Don't think we won't do it. We will," he growled, as his wife got up and slammed the door behind her onto the porch.

"Then do it. Do it," Karl said. "I won't stand idly by when you do, and neither will Nettie, or Christine, and her dad, too—and a whole bunch of us kids who are sick and tired of you fishermen thinking you own the world."

Seth Bunker's face dropped. In Karl's thirteen years, he had never once seen a reaction like this. Then inside, a bubble popped into a little chuckle, rippling and exploding into a laugh. "By gawd, he's a man." He was still laughing when his wife came in and stood beside the table, watching him silently.

Karl had left and didn't hear his father's accolade and the laughter that followed.

15

The Big Traffic Jam

A golden sun flooded Karl's bedroom Thursday morning, forcing him to squint as a fair breeze waltzed along Quarry Cove picking up mixed scents of pine, cedar, and the ever present lavender. He felt invigorated. Being back with Christine was good, and his dad now knew where he stood.

At the window, he stared down the hill toward the pool. All appeared quiet. The pool was full. Lobstermen were rowing their skiffs out to their boats on the moorings. Gulls were getting excited, swirling overhead, screeching and then diving. Across the cove, cars and trucks could be heard faintly as they headed up and down Route 1A.

In the kitchen, he quickly shoveled down cornflakes, grabbed a piece of toast and raced out the door. His mother called after him, "That's no way to eat…"

He coasted down the lane toward Quarry Cove Bridge. A few kids were gathered on the embankment across the cove waiting for the bus.

Jacking the front wheel onto the planked walkway, he slowed his bike, looking down into the calm waters of the pool, empty save for skiffs bobbing at the fishermen's mooring buoys.

He blinked. Then blinked again and stopped. Something bobbed to the surface. Not much of anything. Now instead of a thing, there was bubble…then another, and another.

Suddenly, a squirt of water. Then, that unmistakable orange tinge and smiling blunt face with its flippers raised like a dolphin.

"Bustah!" he said, his voice a half whisper as he swallowed, unable to contain his emotion.

Bustah wiggled his flippers, blinked his tiny eyes, and, as if happy to be recognized, took a nosedive, his flukes waving, before disappearing.

With a snort and a click-clack followed by a fountain out of his blow hole, up popped Bumpah. Immediately, Bustah surfaced alongside her.

A wild cry broke out from the embankment as the throng of kids rushed to the railings cheering and waving.

Both whales must have heard the commotion and immediately started their own chorus of hoots and squeaks as the kids went crazy. Most had vaulted the fence and now gathered on the water's edge waving and shouting:

"Bustah! Bumpah!"

The whales responded with hoots and clicker-clack and penny whistle-like shrieks. Bustah nosedived, the surging water sending a wave to shore, revealing alabaster white skin.

The younger Bumpah followed suit after a loud shriek, a clicker-clack, parting the water and waving his flukes as he disappeared.

The crowd roared. Karl cheered too, as a warm hand gently tightened on his forearm.

"They're back!"

Shaking with excitement, Christine gripped Karl's forearm, pulling herself close to him.

"Great...fantastic...Oh, I don't want to go to school, do you?"

Karl shook his head, as both whales surfaced further down the pool near the neck of the spoon. Two fountains of water shot into the air. Then they dove and scooted back toward the bridge, with the white of Bustah's back showing below the surface, and the reddish tint of Bumpah's skin flashing to the surface.

With a loud roar, the waters parted as both whales surfaced and jibber-jabbered in whale talk intermixed with a gentle smooth hum, like a song.

"Oh my gawd, they're singing," Christine said, clinging even tighter to Karl's arm. He looked at her steel gray eyes sparkling, her face wreathed in happiness, her lips—he couldn't resist it. He kissed her.

Her response was to clasp both hands around his face and press him with a kiss with a smack.

"Take that," she said, laughing, as he felt that mystical warmth surge through his body and eliminate clear thinking.

They were still standing there, laughing and joking as Bustah and Bumpah put on a first class act for an audience that just couldn't get enough.

Even the school bus driver, was enjoying the show as he joined the kids at the railing. Others ran across the bridge to where Karl and Christine held a grandstand view.

Cars and trucks pulled onto the embankment, just as they had on the first day the whales visited. People ran out of their cars, many with cameras ready, as Bustah and Bumpah swam to the railing overlooking the pool and offered the growing crowd their aquatic ballet.

"Look," Christine said, tugging Karl's arm. The police department squad car was pushing through the crowd to the railing on the embankment.

"They must be crazy," Karl said. "They're going to run people over."

The siren whirred, and the red light atop the squad car began to revolve. People moved away as the car continued to push its way to the railing.

Some people started to angrily wave at the driver. He answered them with another whirl of the siren. Infuriated, some fanned out in front of the squad car, facing it head on.

Out of the car stepped Chief Harrington. Leaning over the top of the door, he motioned for the crowd to step aside. In the background, the whales hooted and whistled as the rest of the throng laughed.

"Something's wrong. Where is she?" Karl said as he searched for some sign of Nettie. Christine scanned the crowd with concern.

"There—there she is," said Christine, pointing to Nettie as she was jumping up and down.

There was no mistaking that Nettie's resolute stance as she stood facing the chief, hands on hips, not budging. The Chief's jaw moved mechanically, obviously angered at her posture.

Grabbing their bikes, Karl and Christine swung their legs over the seats, swerving and wobbling through the ever increasing crowd on the bridge.

Tourists aimed cameras, kids hollered, and there were shrieks of excitement as Bustah and Bumpah staged an encore.

Christine and Karl dropped their bikes in the only clear spot they could find, near some cedar bushes at the end of the bridge. They grabbed their backpacks and struggled to get through the wall of noisy people.

"Well, then, you're just going to do what a lot of people want you to do?" Nettie's voice rolled over the heads of the throng. The crowd cheered.

"Don't ya push it, or, don't ya think I will," the chief growled back, as Karl and Christine edged through the crowd which was now booing the Chief.

"Nettie?" Christine cried out through the noise.

Nettie heard her and waved. The crowd turned, and Christine and Karl forced their way through the gap.

Nettie flung her arms around their shoulders.

"Our babies are back," Nettie said, happily.

The Chief scowled as the crowd cheered again, almost drowned out amid the wild splashing as Bustah and Bumpah frolicked.

"You kids better get on that bus and get off to school," the Chief said, glaring at Karl and Christine.

"You're going to need a driver," Nettie said with a laugh. The Chief shook his head when he saw Elwood Tinker hooting and hollering down at the railing. Angrily, he spun around and managed to weave his way back to the car.

"I'm glad you kids could make it. We're having a whale of a good time," said Nettie. She and the crowd around her laughed.

"The Chief's getting madder and madder," Christine said.

"Let him. It won't do him any g—"

"This is Chief Harrington," the metallic voice interrupted the air over the squad car speaker.

"This is Chief Harrington," he repeated. "I'm asking all of you people to move back from the railing."

"Why? What's the matter with that guy? Aw, nuts," a disgruntled sightseer cried out. Some men and women faced the squad car, defiant, with faces drawn, while some shook their heads in disapproval.

Nettie stifled a laugh, shaking her head, while Karl and Christine laughed.

"If he isn't careful, he'll have a riot on his hands," Nettie said.

"This is Chief—"

"Ah, shuddup," a short burly man in mechanic's overalls with "Charlie" scrawled in red ribbon over his chest pocket, growled, waving the Chief's message aside.

His buddy, a tall skinny man with an oily cap clinging to a crop of red hair and "Red" over his breast pocket, stretched gum around his mouth and gave the chief an uncomplimentary forearm gesture.

"Oh, no," Nettie said, inching through the crowd to the man. "Please. Don't provoke him. He's ready to arrest someone."

"Then let him come and take me in," Red said, as his buddy Charlie chuckled.

"Ain't got no sense," Charlie said. "What could two whales do to cause this flap?"

"He wants to shoot them," Nettie said, seizing an opportunity to gain new allies.

"Then he's going to have to shoot us first—ain't he, Red?"

Blue lights flashed above two state police cruisers as they drew up. Chief Harrington quickly slipped out of his squad car and strode over to them.

Two tall troopers dwarfed the Chief as they stepped onto the embankment. Nettie edged through the crowd, Karl and Christine in tow.

"Send for reinforcements," Red shouted, bringing another cheer from the crowd. The troopers smiled as they tried to hear the Chief.

"The only thing we can do is make sure the highway is not blocked, Chief," one trooper said.

"Not much you can do if the people just want to watch the whales," the other said.

"They're causing a disturbance," Chief Harrington said, swinging around almost colliding with Nettie.

"That's ridiculous and you know it," Nettie said, as the troopers looked at her.

"She's the one, this one," the Chief said. "She's causing all the trouble. She's inciting these people to riot."

The troopers exchanged puzzled glances and shook their heads.

"The only thing we can do, Chief, is get the drivers to pull over more so that traffic can move freely down 1A."

One trooper slipped behind the wheel of his cruiser and reached for his mike.

"May I have your attention, please?" A hush fell over the crowd, save for the splashing of Bustah and Bumpah. Then, even they stopped their antics.

"Some of your cars are parked too close to the main road for travel," the trooper continued. "If you would kindly pull them closer to the side of the highway, it would be much appreciated."

Some of the spectators walked to their vehicles. A man with a semitrailer gave the troopers a high sign as he passed.

"Pull it in closer," the trooper shouted.

"I got to be off," the driver shouted back. "Have a nice day."

The trooper raised his hand in a salute. Other drivers were moving their cars in closer, pulling as far to the side of the road as possible.

The bus driver strode up through the thinning crowd.

"Be a lot better if we can get that bus out of here, too," the trooper said.

"On my way," the driver answered. "Would you tell the kids the bus is about to leave?"

The officer made the announcement and a bunch of kids disentangled themselves from the railing and the bridge overpass, walking slowly to the bus.

"We'd better go. Will you be alright?" Christine asked.

Nettie smiled. "Of course...everything's under control for now," she said, clasping her hands on Christine's shoulders.

"I'll stay if you want me to," Karl said. But Nettie just shook her head, hugged his shoulders and thanked him. Christine latched onto Karl's arm and steered him toward the bus.

"I'm glad we're all on the same wavelength," she said, flashing him a big grin.

16

Tripper Gets Hooked

Morning assembly started off with Principal Brown marching across the wooden floor, her high stiletto heels clicking like little hammer taps.

"I want all students here to know that there is a serious situation brewing at the pool now that the whales have returned." She scanned the hall, ears cocked for any comment, her face taut, her eyes narrowed.

"It's been brought to my attention that some of you are creating problems with the police." She paused, her head uncomfortably rolling around.

Some students scoffed. But Christine was already on her feet and Karl stood up with her.

"Miss Brown, that's simply not true." The Principal was taken back, and looked across the stage to where Roger Millett sat. He started to stand, but Miss Brown urged him to remain seated.

"I am reporting what the police are telling me," she said, her voice almost shrill, as she swallowed, shaking her head.

"The police know better than that," Karl said, as Christine's fingers tightened on his forearm.

"It's not just we who are attracted to the whales, people are coming down from all over the place," he said.

"We're not doing anything to hinder the police," Christine said. "They're just trying to keep the traffic rolling on 1A."

"Stirring up trouble, too," Tripper Gleason scoffed from behind them.

Karl turned as Gleason stood up and scowled at them.

"You two are the ring leaders, along with that Beal woman from the lighthouse, an' my dad says she ought to be run out of town…"

A roar of disapproval filled the hall.

"Sit down, Gleason…why don't you shut up and let people speak…" several students cried out.

Roger Millett was on his feet as Principal Brown's face turned sunset red and she stepped back from the podium.

"This is not a court," Millet shouted above the roar. "All of you sit down—now!"

The mumble evaporated.

"This is not a court, neither is it an inquisition. You know what that is, Mr. Gleason?"

Gleason's cheeks reddened as he groaned and sat back in his chair. The students next to him shuffled uneasily.

Millett waited for complete silence.

"I believe that Principal Brown is trying to tell you that your cooperation with the police will be appreciated," he said, turning to Miss Brown.

She nodded in agreement.

"Of course, I have heard that some of you were protesting at the town meeting the other night," she said.

Millett raised his eyebrows and whispered into her ear. She coughed uncomfortably at what he said, then flashed a quick smile and continued.

"I know you all have a right to express yourselves on any issue confronting our local government. All I'm asking is that you present yourselves in a respectful manner worthy of that befitting the students at Pepper Mill High School."

Gleason groaned and raised his hand. Miss Brown smiled and beckoned him to stand.

"All I was tryin' to say was that some students here are protesting—waving signs, upsetting the selectmen's meeting, and interfering with the police. An' not only that, but the lobstermen too…"

Millett took the podium again, bidding Gleason to take his seat, as the students moaned.

"As I said before, this is not an inquisition where we find students guilty of things not associated with this school," Millett said as Miss Brown lowered her head to hide her anger, her shoe heels scraping the floor.

"Any problems with the presence of the whales has to be dealt with by the Sea and Shore Wardens. This is not something that calls for unilateral decision-making on any one group's part. I'm sure reason will triumph over recklessness here. Meanwhile, anyone who wishes to demonstrate in support of the whales," he paused and looked over the hall, "is free to do so."

Millett stepped back smiling, as the auditorium full of students roared their approval.

Christine and Karl rose with the rest of the cheering students, as Gleason and his toadies growled and strutted out of the hall.

"You'd better watch your step," Gleason muttered as he passed Karl. "Her, too," he added, jerking his finger toward Christine.

Karl hauled back and landed his right under Gleason's lantern jaw, and jerked his fist back with an, "Ow!"

Gleason stood stunned. His eyes floated. Then, like a tall tree with the last cut made, he fell flat on his back.

An ear-splitting roar filled the auditorium.

No amount of excuses would change Principal Brown's decision to suspend Karl for five days. She sat high in her elevated chair behind a desk decorated with ceramic cats and a picture of her hugging her Maine Coon cat. Millett, as usual, stood nervously to one side, his face expressionless.

"So, that's that," Miss Brown said. "Report to Mr. Millett for instructions." she said, shaking her head irritably. Millett nodded Karl toward a chair, as he slumped into the seat behind his desk.

"Why?" he asked. "Why did you have to go and do that?" he said, shaking his head, looking for a suspension form amid stacks of books and files.

"He threatened Christine and me," Karl said. Millett paused, fumbling through the papers and files, and looked at him.

"What kind of threat?"

"Told me I'd better watch it...and Christine too, just after you finished speaking."

Millett shook his head. "You should have come and told me instead of dropping him with that right— ever think of boxing? Besides, telling you to 'watch it,' doesn't necessarily constitute a physical threat... now, does it?"

"He's always threatening. The other day, he just came over and started kicking the stuffin' out of me."

"Yeah, what was that all about anyway...the same thing? These whales?"

Karl nodded.

"I'll see what I can do...can't promise...but...a week's a long time to be out."

"Sure appreciate it, Mr. Millett," Karl said as Millett completed the form and passed a carbon copy to him.

17

Bows and Arrows

Karl began a half jog for the four-mile run home. There would be no reprieve. Millett gave him two thumbs down as he closed the door to Miss Brown's office.

Alongside Granite Ledge Lake, which stretched for two miles on the other side of Dingle's Rock, he stood fascinated as a blue and white sloop sailed past, leisurely heading to Spaulding's dock at the far end of the lake in Pepper Mill Cove. An older man, with a pipe and a Red Sox ball cap squashed down on a mop of gray hair, relaxed behind the tiller. Gently raising his hand, Karl smiled and waved back.

Once more he took off around Dingle Rock. It was a little windy down Slate Road as he entered the downhill stretch to Quarry Cove Bridge.

A few people were leaning over the railing staring at the pool, and Joe Mullins was standing next to his cruiser. Quickly he dropped his cigarette, heeling it into the gravel. Seeing Karl, he did a double take.

"Out early?" he started. Karl just nodded, then ran toward the railing. Larry Greenfield, the farmer, leaned back, and pushed the string of his long bow forward, a brown feathered arrow between his thumb and forefinger, sighting in on an imaginary target in the pool.

"Hey...hey...stop! Whadya think you're doing?" he shouted, as Greenfield lowered the bow.

"Getting ready," the stocky farmer replied. "Good hunting hereabouts, heh?" He reached into the back of the pickup and lifted a homemade harpoon. It was a broomstick with a spearhead knotted on the point. A thin string of clothesline ran down the shaft where the remainder of the cord was knotted.

His son and daughter held up their own bows and laughed. A quiver of arrows was slung around their shoulders.

"What's up, Karl?" his equally stocky son Darrell said as his sister Belinda moved close, a smile stretched across her mouth. "Why don't ya get your bow and let's have some fun with these porkers."

"Are you kidding?" Karl said. Angrily, he pushed aside Belinda's bow and spun around to see what Joe Mullins was doing. Mullins was dragging on another cigarette. He blew out a stream of blue smoke and raised his hand.

"Are you going to just stand there and let these people shoot these whales with their bows and arrows?"

Mullins quickly tossed his cigarette to the ground, rubbed his heel on the butt, shrugged his shoulders, and walked over to Karl.

"Now, Karl, they ain't doing anything, are ya folk?"

"Not yet, haven't surfaced for a while. But wait until they do, we'll be waiting. Won't we, kids?" Larry Greenfield said with his round red face beaming from beneath a brown Greenfield's Milk cap.

"What?" Karl said, staring unbelievably at Greenfield and shaking his head. "You can't do that. These whales are protected."

"Yeah?" said Darrell. "Who in hell's name is going to protect whales?"

"I am," said Karl, staring straight into Darrell's face. There was a pause, and then Darrell's mouth twitched as he broke into a laugh. He looked at Belinda, who snickered with embarrassment.

"You mean you going to try and stop us?" Darrell said, chuckling and switching glances between his dad and Mullins. "Ya got to be kiddin', Karl. Are ya nuts or something?"

"You tell 'em, Joe," Karl said, looking for some support from the patrolman who stood quietly listening to the exchange.

Joe coughed a little and tried to get a word out, but faltered.

"Well, we can't do much..."

"Oh, no? Well I can." Nettie latched onto Karl's arm and centered herself between them. Mullins looked shocked—even scared—and stiffened, spluttering a little as he stood back.

"I'm telling you, and you'd better listen to me, Larry Greenfield," she said, waving one of her long piano fingers in front of the startled farmer's nose. "If you as much as lift a finger to harm Bustah and Bumpah, you'll be raking hay with one hand."

Greenfield looked shocked, and then started to chuckle. "Oh, fer gawd's sake, c'mon Nettie, we're only just going to have a little fun."

"You'll think haying with one hand is fun," she said, pointing that long index back into his face. "Get out of here with those bows and arrows. Go play Robin Hood someplace else."

Rebuked, Greenfield looked crestfallen. His son and daughter looked to him hoping for some encouragement. With none coming, they lowered their heads like chastised children.

"You should know better," Nettie said, swinging around to Joe Mullins, who was startled by her confrontation. "Just standing here and letting those people shoot arrows into two defenseless whales, eh? What's wrong with you?"

With a red face, Mullins stood speechless as the Greenfields walked back to their pickup, their heads down, and Belinda dragging her bow.

Karl watched as they noisily dropped their bows and arrow quills into the back of the truck and Greenfield walked to the driver's side.

"Getting to be something, when ya can't hunt anymore," Greenfield shouted across the parking lot as he climbed into the cab and banged the door. "It won't be long before they stop ya from using mouse traps."

"Hunt?" Nettie yelled at him stamping her sneakers into the graveled lot. "Hunt?"

With both hands on the open window hatch, she looked with disgust at Greenfield and his two children who stared at her in disbelief.

"Why don't you go hunt a cow? Now that's hunting. Real hunting."

Greenfield's face was a blank as he sat there with his hands in his lap.

Nettie stepped back, and Greenfield cranked the engine nervously into first as Nettie stared defiantly after him, hands on her hips, her sneakers dug in the gravel. She stood there until she saw the truck round the curve above Cove Bridge and then disappear toward Pepper Mill.

Karl's face glowed in admiration as Nettie spun around and marched determinedly toward Joe Mullins.

"As for you, Joe Mullins, you ought to be damned well ashamed of yourself."

Mullins swallowed hard, sucked in some air and prepared to answer.

"Call yourself an officer of the law, and you're standing there watching as those big game hunters shoot two harmless whales."

"But, Nettie," he started. She stopped within inches of him, completely fearless, as Karl struggled to keep a straight face. Thin as a pencil, short brown hair, and a sharp lean face that hid a gentle heart, Nettie Beal held fort.

"If anything happens to those whales, you're going to be one sorry policeman."

"Now that's a threat," Mullins's voice trembled.

"Look here, Joe Mullins. Call it a threat if you like, but if anything happens to those whales while you're standing here puffing on your cigarettes and enjoying this charade, you will be one unhappy man."

"Now that's a threat, that is," Mullins said, jerking his head back in shock. "You heard it, didn't you Karl?" he said, searching for support from Karl, who was having trouble keeping a straight face and just shrugged his shoulders.

"I'm going to charge you with threatening a police officer," Mullins said marching off to his cruiser, with Nettie directly behind him.

"You don't get it, do you, Joe?" Nettie said as he squeezed behind the wheel and looked for his summons book. Turning, he looked up at her. "Would you like to be known as that Maine police officer who stood idly by as people slaughtered two harmless whales?"

Mullins just sat there, lost for words.

"What do you think visitors will say when they pass through Quarry Cove and Pepper Mill? 'Oh, look! This is where that town cop let people kill two whales'," she said, mimicking a tourist. "You know you won't be working for the police department when that happens.

Mullins flinched and hastily put his summons book down.

"Well, they weren't doing anything…" he started, as Karl approached.

"But they were about to," Karl said, as Nettie draped her arm over his shoulder. "Besides, it's breaking the law to hunt within town limits." Nettie's fingers tightened.

"But this is a bit different, ain't it? I mean, whales ain't like deer or bear…?"

"Doesn't matter whether it's a bear or deer, there's a No Hunting sign over there by the bridge," Nettie said. "So, I would imagine that means no hunting. Doesn't matter whether it's fox, bear, deer, skunk, rabbits, and whales. You can't hunt here."

Mullins face tightened and he nodded his head. "Well, I s'pose yer right on that," he said. "Sign is up over there. I'd forgotten that. Thanks for reminding me."

"So? Where's my summons?" Nettie said. Mullins waved his hands in frustration.

"Ah, forget it. I just thought you were threatening me with bodily harm—an' that would have been a serious offense." He looked up at Nettie, expecting a reply, but she just smiled.

"You'll never know," she said, "will you?"

Turning, she waltzed across the parking lot with Karl beside her. Mullins answered his radio, started the cruiser, and swung out of the lot heading toward Lookout Point.

Ripples of water washed over the embankment, but the pool was quiet. A family from away leaned on the rail. The young man had a camera dangling around his neck. His five-year-old son and an older daughter were running up and along the rail laughing and shouting. Their mother, a slim young lady with auburn hair, stood smiling and waiting.

A huge white foaming wave split the waters in the cove as Bustah and Bumpah surfaced, then plunged back into the pool. Shouts of surprise riveted the family against the rail as the father struggled frantically to get the camera strap from around his neck.

The children pressed their faces against the railing.

"Oh, my gosh!" cried the woman, her mouth wide open. Her children stopped dead in their tracks.

"Oh, look, Daddy!" shouted the little girl. Her brother let out a "Wow!" and gripped the railing, awaiting the next plunge.

"Isn't that great?" Nettie called out, as the father fussed with the lens on his Canon, readjusted, aimed, and waited.

"I can't believe it," shouted the mother, turning toward Nettie. "However did you get them to come up here?"

Bustah and Bumpah rolled just below the surface, and the family quickly turned to face the pool.

"They're just visiting," Nettie said, happily staring across the pool.

"Wished we had something like this at home," the boy said.

"Me, too," his sister said. "How do we get them to do this, daddy?"

"We don't, honey. They are wild mammals. They love the sea and that's where they belong."

Both whales, as if on cue, did a smooth half-surface role, blew out some water, and followed with a sweet song and Bumpah's click-click-clackety-clack. The children screamed with delight.

In an extraordinary show, the whales raised their heads above the water a few feet offshore. The kids went wild. Bustah appeared to be sitting with his flippers on top of the water. His tiny eyes shone with delight, and he opened his beak and delivered a mellow song.

Bumpah broke surface, snuggled up to Bustah, and showed off a mouthful of sharp, glistening white teeth, followed by a clickety-click-clack.

"They look more like dolphins," the woman said, "especially with their snouts."

Her husband was busily clicking the Canon's shutter and cranking the film as fast as his thumb would go.

"Come on, baby, oh, come on. Give me another one. That's it, that's it. Ooh, baby, that's beautiful…Smile…Hold it there, that's it."

Karl could hardly hold back his laughter. Nettie exchanged glances with him and squeezed his elbow, just the way Christine did. But then her face turned somber.

"They've got to go, Karl. They have to."

"But, why?"

"They're getting too friendly," she said, somewhat depressed.

"You should keep them here," the young man said, still clicking the shutter. "We've never seen anything like it. What a show."

"I'd love that," Nettie said, her face gleaming. "Love it. Oh, my gosh, wouldn't I love to have Bustah and Bumpah stay here forever."

"Hey Bustah," shouted the boy.

"Come on, Bumpah," shouted his sister.

"Bustah and Bumpah—fantastic. They have names?" the man asked.

His wife clasped her hands together. "I love it," she cried out. "Love it."

A lobster boat rounded Mollusk Point letting out a puff of black smoke as the lobsterman throttled his engine back. Nettie's fingers dug into Karl's arm.

Like ghosts, the Belugas silently slipped below the surface, leaving just a few ripples and a short gasp of air bubbles trailing and dotting the surface above their orange-colored heads.

"Oh, no, what happened?" the man said, dropping his hands. He took in Nettie's hard look and followed her stare across the pond to the boat. His kids looked dejected as their mother tried to console them.

"Is it them?" he said, pointing a finger at the boat, as yet another boat rounded the point.

"They fear for the fish," Nettie said. "They want to kill them."

"You've got to be kidding? What? Are you for real?" he went on, shaking his head in disbelief. His wife's face turned gloomy as she put her hands on her children's shoulders and moved them along the fence out of range.

But it was too late. They'd already heard. The girl started to cry. Then, with both tiny fists in her eyes, she started to sob. Her brother's face was covered in tears as he tried to look brave, stifling a sob, and turned away embarrassed.

Nettie apologized. "What I should have said is that they want to. But they ain't about to as long as Nettie Beal's here...oh, and my very good...best friends, Karl Bunker and Christine Alley."

She searched the lot, then looked back at Karl.

"How come you're out of school? Where's Christine?"

She listened tensely as he quickly explained, and she assured him everything would be all right.

The lobstermen were in their skiffs dipping their oars in and out of the water in short strokes making their way to the float on the Quarry Hill side of the pool. Karl followed one skiff as the lobsterman, his father, stared back at him.

"Don't worry," Nettie said. "Tell him what happened, he'll understand."

Karl scoffed, shaking his head. His father was standing on the float staring across at him as he coiled some green trap cord. He'd stop, look, and then look again, not quite sure if it was his son. Disgustedly, he flipped his hand half-heartedly and Karl waved, too.

The students spilled noisily out of the school bus, followed by Elwood Tinker, who strode quickly to the fence, waving to Karl and Nettie. Karl looked around, searching for Christine.

"Over there," Nettie said, nodding toward Christine standing on the bottom step of the bus looking across the gathering crowd. Seeing him, she quickly waved and ran toward him.

"Whoopie," cried the kids as Karl wrapped his arms around Christine and they exchanged a quick kiss.

Of course, she already knew what had happened.

"Principal Brown is a nerd," she said. "If Ryan had done that to you, she would have said it was your fault. How's it going? I'm famished."

Waving to the family who still stood at the railing, it was Nettie's promise of Johnny's Finest Kind sandwiches and fresh lemonade that sent the trio racing madly across Quarry Cove Bridge, kicking up the dust as they scurried along Mollusk Point Causeway to Nettie's home.

Inside her kitchen, Nettie lost no time pouring glasses of fresh lemonade and slicing the Italian sandwiches in front of her friends. They eagerly tucked into the feast with gusto, Karl savoring an extra helping of tangy, eye-smarting onions heaped on his sandwich by Christine. Christine stuck out her tongue and grimaced as Nettie chuckled.

There seemed no end to recounting what had happened in the day. Nettie related her experience of a near arrest by Joe Mullins, and about she and Karl accosting the Greenfield farmers which moved Christine to snuggle up to Karl and peck his cheek. He turned to kiss her back, but she pulled back.

"Not with all those onions!"

"Now, all we have to do is face tomorrow...," Nettie started.

"And tonight—" Karl interrupted, his smile fading.

"Everything's going to be okay..." Nettie said. "It is...at least, I hope it is…"

They all exchanged glances and broke out in uproarious laughter.

18

Working the Stern

Later, with supper eaten and the dishes cleared from the table, Karl's father leaned back in his chair with his palms pressed together and stared hard at Karl. His mother had already blamed Tripper for the fight, and his father readily agreed.

"I don't like all this threatening that's going on," he said.

"I know," his mother said. "This used to be a real friendly village. Now we've got everyone threatening everyone else."

"Need ya on the stern tomorrow...no sense sitting around here, or hanging 'round the pool...might as well go out with me every day until this is over."

"What about Saturday?" Karl asked.

"What about it?" his father said. "Still a good day for haulin', as a fella says."

"He's just had that set aside for the annual regatta," his mother said, leaning on her husband's shoulders. "Surely you can spare him for one day?"

Seth Bunker shook his head.

"Regatta? Is that all ya got on your mind, along with them whales?"

"Come on, dad, be a sport. Remember, you're the one who bought him the dinghy," his mother said as she shuffled plates and mugs together and put them in the sink.

His dad stretched, shook his head at his son, and stood up.

"Oh, alright...but..."

Karl and his mother waited.

"But jest as long as ya stay away from that pool, and...that Nettie Beal."

Karl started to speak as his mother held his shoulders and his dad walked out of the kitchen into the parlor to turn on the news.

"Well, you're okay for the regatta...that's one up..."

"I can't stop seeing Nettie...and I won't."

"Shhh," his mother said, placing a finger to her lips, "one thing at a time. He'll get over it, don't you worry...you'll see. Best not to say anything when your dad's like this," she said smiling at him, "I know."

19

Nettie Jailed

Karl lost little time coasting down Quarry Cove Hill. Christine yelled to him as she pedaled across Cove Bridge and he ran to meet her.

"Have you heard?" she said all out of breath.

Dismounting, she let the bike drop onto the gravel, ignoring his attempt to catch it because it was brand new.

"It's Nettie," she started. "Chief Harrington has arrested her." Karl's mouth fell open – "Charged her with threatening."

"But I was there," Karl jumped in. "Joe Mullins ignored what she said."

"Wasn't Mullins," Christine said. "It was Larry Greenfield. Guess she threatened to take off his arm if he harpooned the whales." She started to laugh.

"She told Larry what she meant. She was upset. She didn't mean anything...oh, I don't know—she was pretty angry. But how did the Chief get wind of it?"

"That's not all," a wide-eyed Christine continued, anxious to tell him everything. "She's heard there's a move on to get the Coast Guard to get her out of her house."

"What? I don't believe it," Karl said, as they walked toward the bridge. "How? I mean, how can you lose your house just because you like whales?"

"She was the assistant lighthouse keeper," Christine said. "When Phil passed on, she automatically became the keeper."

"So they can't do anything, then, can they?"

"They'll try. They'll do their best to get rid of her. I heard they claimed she was incompetent."

"That's a laugh…why, the light's never shone brighter. She keeps it polished and the house and grounds—just like she did when Phil was there. It just doesn't make sense."

Christine chuckled. "Perhaps it's because she's a woman."

"What's that got to do with it?" Karl said, hunching his shoulders.

Christine smiled, staring straight into his face. "It has a lot to do with it…a lot more than you think."

Christine turned away, her head lowered. She leaned over the railing looking down at the two huge whales with their unmistakable orange caps on, as a tiny stream of bubbles swirled to the surface.

"How happy they are," she said, as Karl rested his hand on hers.

"Do you believe that…you know…'cause she's a woman?"

"Could be," she said, turning, a smile crossing her face. "Look around you. All a girl has to look forward to when she gets out of high school is a clerk's job or some petty soda fountain jerk…and getting married, having kids, or knitting heads for lobster traps."

The parking lot was already full and Joe Mullins was keeping a line of 1A traffic moving, and directing whale watchers to pull in closer to the curb.

"Tell me something," Christine said, staring into Karl's face, her steel gray eyes penetrating his soul and washing away all resistance. "Tell me..."

"What?" he said.

"Do you...oh, never mind."

"Tell me. Come on tell me," he urged. She continued to walk across the bridge as he badgered her to finish her question. She just strode ahead, struggling to hide a smile. Her mom was always talking about how boys have a hard time showing their feelings. Karl was no exception, she thought.

There was excited and wild arm thumping for Karl and warm hugs for Christine, as the kids poured off the bus and surrounded the pair.

"Go get 'em, Tiger," some of the boys yelled excitedly, clamoring around Karl. They roared approval when he shouted "Regatta," and thumped their forearms high in a salute. Another wild cry and whistles erupted when he grasped Christine's arm and yelled "First Mate."

"Saturday," cried Christine. "We need everyone." The crowd let out another "Whoo" and did a double stomp in the gravel parking lot to show their support.

Joe Mullins moved closer, a cigarette dangling from his lips, his arms waving outward trying to get the crowd to move back from the railing. "That railing ain't going to hold all of you people pushing on it," he said, in his best John Wayne style, eyebrows furrowed and chin tucked in. "Keep pushing and y'all be in the pool with them whales. Then y'all find out they ain't as playful as them seem."

Karl turned and faced him.

"I thought...," he started, as Mullins held up his palm.

"Ain't me buddy, not me. It was the Greenfields that reported her – that's who it was...I could have taken her in for what she said to me...but she's in enough trouble already—an' ya know somethin'? It's her fault. She threatened to take his arm off, she did." His face tensed seeing the growing crowd, and he walked back to his cruiser, which was surrounded by sightseers. "B'sides, I ain't got time to get a smoke with these whales and Nettie doing her thing."

"But where is she?" Christine said, craning to see over the heads of the crowd.

"I don't believe him...don't believe him," Karl said, staring after Mullins. "I've known the Greenfields for years, they're not like that – especially Larry. Remember when he found us all on his haystack?"

"He was more concerned about us smoking than anything else," Christine said. "I think you're right. I can't see Larry doing something like that, any more than Darrell and Belinda."

The crowd was cheering, hooting and hollering in an attempt to get Bustah and Bumpah to entertain them. But for a few bubbles and the wash of water over the rocks as the tide started to ebb, nothing stirred.

"Bustah," a deep voice roared.

"Bumpah," another shouted.

There was a pause, a quiet reflection by the crowd, and then the crowd of men, women and children joined in a synchronized chant.

"Bustah, Bumpah, Bustah…"

They clapped their hands in a steady beat to accompany the chant.

Christine and Karl joined in, but nothing stirred beneath the rapidly receding tide. Bustah and Bumpah were settling down for the night in a thick, blackish brown, velvety soft bed of Quarry Cove mud.

"We've got to find Nettie," Christine said, scanning the crowd.

"There, she is," said Karl. "Look, she just got out of that car by the road. Come on!"

He grabbed Christine's hand as they pushed through the sightseers.

"Meet our new friends," Nettie said, her face wreathed in happiness.

"Allow me to introduce you to Mr. and Mrs. Irving Schubert of Boston…and you know what? They bailed me out of Chief Harrison's dungeon.

Irving Schubert emerged from the car a wide smile on his face, as he extended his hand, and his wife and two children followed. It was the same family he had met earlier.

"That's exactly what it was – a dungeon," Schubert said, gripping Karl's hand and patting his shoulder, as his wife clasped Christine's hand warmly. "A dungeon? Well, I don't know about that – but..." He chuckled and shook his head, "They had no right doing that to this lady," he said. "Furthermore, it makes me mad to think they're trying to bounce her out of her home."

"Who told the Chief?" Christine asked, anxiously awaiting Nettie's reply. "Who was it? Come on—"

"I'll tell you one day, but not now," Nettie said.

The Schuberts had spotted Nettie being driven across the bridge from the lighthouse in the police cruiser. They'd followed it to the station at Pepper Mill, where First Selectman and local justice Chauncey Philpot set Nettie's bail at five dollars. Schubert swiftly dropped the money on the judge's podium, then graciously waited as Chauncey Philpot read from his notes, cautioning Nettie about what would happen if she failed to appear before him on Monday.

"Mr. Schubert will forfeit his bail, and you will have to go back into jail," he warned, his eyes wide, fearful of imposing such consequences.

"Seems the Chief has his own jail," Nettie said with a grin. "He's put bars on a backroom window in what used to be his garage, and nailed a clasp lock on the door. Anyone could bust out."

They all laughed.

"I could have done that, too, and was about to, had it not been for these lovely people. Hey, look who's back," said Nettie, pointing to Johnny's white luncheon wagon gaudily decorated with flags that inched into the lot behind the spectators.

Yankee Doodle Dandy blared from speakers atop the driver's cab.

"Johnny's Finest Kind!" Nettie said, rubbing her hands together. "Come on, let's get something to eat."

"Bet you're glad the whales are back," Nettie said to a cheerful Johnny.

"You betcha," Johnny chuckled, nodding his head as he cut a sandwich in two, wrapped it in white paper and handed it to an eager young boy straining on his toes to see the top of the counter.

"Hope they stick around for a while – Bangor and Blue Hill Fairs both sometime away. I need unexpected things like this," Johnny said, as he spooned some nose-pinching and eye-watering onions into an open roll, sniffing approvingly.

"Got the regatta this Saturday and that should help—along with the boat show in Belfast next week."

They all ate the nearly foot-long ham, pepperoni, provolone cheese and onion delight as they perched on a picnic table.

The pool was almost empty except for where the whales had found a mud bed in the deep end of the pool. They were now snuggled up close to each other. Only the orange spots on the tops of their heads and the white of their gigantic bodies could be seen as the water swirled over their heads.

They finished their sandwiches and then stood in the middle of the bridge. Nettie stared down into the water. Karl and Christine stood beside her, along with the Schubert family. Their children anxiously scanned the cloudy waters trying to see the whales.

"Come on...come on...where are you? No time to sleep," Nettie urged softly. Pursing her lips, she gave out a strange deep moan, which sounded much akin to the whale sounds Karl and Christine had heard.

Again she blew a long low tone as everyone stared at the inert forms below.

Shaking her head, she inhaled deeply, blew out, laughed, and tried again.

"Whoodle-ah-whoodle-e-o. Ah – clickety-click-clacker clack."

There was a gurgle, almost like someone pulling a plunger out of a stopped-up sink, a loud gush of water and a pop, and Bustah and Bumpah took a bow. The crowd went wild. Yells and cheers filled the air. Some blew their car horns, and flashed their lights.

Wide-eyed with surprise at the sight of two big plump whales sitting up in the muddy water staring up at the bridge knocked everyone back. People froze – mesmerized – as the two whales leaned back in the water, as though in rocking chairs, their jaws wide open smiling up at the bridge.

"There you are, my lovelies," Nettie said, tears twinkling in the corner of her eyes as she blew them kisses. The whales seemed to hum, paused, and then followed with a clicker-click-clack as they snapped their teeth together.

Schubert's 8-mm movie camera whirred.

"Oh, my gawd," he stammered unable to control his delight, as his wife excitedly clenched her fists together and their two children jumped up and down shouting with delight. Karl looked into Christine's smiling face, throwing his arm around her waist and pulling her close.

"Whoo –ooh," Nettie started again.

Bustah and Bumpah responded with in a soft, mellow tone that was almost a moan. It was all Nettie needed to hear as she stood there choked up with joy. Christine and Karl walked over, and put their arms around Nettie.

"They always look like they're smiling," Christine said, as Bumpah blinked or winked. The two appeared perfectly relaxed, leaning back, big grins across their faces, and holding their flippers up on each side of their heads like hands. Their short snouts opened and closed, showing off a mouthful of sharp and impeccable white teeth.

20

A Lull Before the Storm

Thursday night was full of hustle and bustle to get fishing boot waders, thick woolen gray socks, and yellow oilskins ready for what Karl called the 'bait baggers ordeal.'

"Could do worse," his dad said. "Sure beats an office job shuffling papers. You could end up like Chauncey Philpot. Poor ol' Chauncey, sitting in a bank all these years."

They tucked into the flounder topped with paisley sauce Karl's mom had made. She moved deftly between the stove and table ladling out French fries when one flipped out of the pan.

"Good catch that," she said.

"Too bad my son doesn't dangle a line off the dock and catch one," his dad said, chewing away, salting and dousing his fries with vinegar. "Then again, won't be many flounder left if them whales don't leave."

It had to happen. Karl knew it would. Silently he ate and waited.

"I see you're not paying any attention to what I said about dallying around with that crew."

"What crew?"

"Why, that Christine and Nettie gal. Hear they jailed her?"

"She's out," Karl snapped back. "And, Christine ain't just a 'crew'."

"Come on, you two," Karl's mom said. "This whole thing will straighten out...you wait an' see. Besides, Seth, that Christine is a real pretty girl, and very nice, too."

Seth Bunker coughed and lowered his head.

"It's that Nettie that gets me," he said. "Anyone'd think them whales was her pets."

"She just loves animals...that's all there is to it," Laura Bunker said, shuffling the plates together and walking to the sink.

21

Scuttling the *Clamshell*

The next morning, a throng of school kids waiting for the bus had brought loaves of bread with them. Some were rolling the bread into balls and slinging them like baseball pitchers to the whales. Bumpah nudged one, lowered his jaw and the bread ball floated into his mouth. The kids on the bridge yelled encouragement.

"Karl...they're still here," Christine said running to him across the bridge, as he sloshed in his heavy sea boots behind his father along the gravel path toward the float.

"See ya later," Karl called, as his dad mumbled. Christine blew him a kiss, waved, and he awkwardly sent one back making sure his dad didn't see him.

"Take care," she called, and Karl waved back again.

"Women...boy, they sure do fuss," Seth Bunker said, climbing into the skiff.

Karl picked up the oars and started to row toward the *Laura,* his dad's boat.

"Looks like she's takin' on some water," his dad said, nodding toward Karl's dinghy tied up at the next float. "Pull over, let's take a look."

"Cork's out," his dad said, holding the gunwale as Karl drew up alongside his fourteen-foot day sailor.

"Bail 'er out an' I'll come back for ya."

Karl took a large coffee can and stepped into the flooded cockpit of his lapstrake boat. Pushing the boom aside, he screwed the brass plug back into the center board housing, and vigorously scooped out the water.

He was almost finished when the prow of the *Laura* silently rubbed up alongside him. Dropping the can, he rolled over onto the deck as his dad backed the boat into the channel. Black smoke swirled atop the cuddy and water swished around the stern, while the seagulls screamed for breakfast.

Morning went fast. The *Laura* sprinted between the red-topped buoys, Seth Bunker taking a turn on the winch with the trap rope, and hauling the trap amidships. Once his dad had cleared the trap of lobsters and some cod, Karl would quickly unwrap the bait bag cord from around the wooden lathes, pull out the empty bait bag, reach into the bait barrel, scoop in handfuls of soaked brown herring, tie it back in the trap, and close the trap.

It went on like that all morning.

They were with but four strings of traps left to haul, when his dad idled the engine and wiped his gloves on the exhaust sending out a cloud of steam with a pungent whiff of salt water.

"Let's eat."

Peeling his gloves off, Karl swished his swollen, red hands in the sea, gulped some fresh air, and strode up under the cuddy, where his dad unwrapped a loaf of bread and handed Karl a can of sardines.

Together, they stood feet apart staring straight ahead as the boat slowly rolled and was lifted in the small swell. Legs apart, they braced as they stuffed sardines and bread into their mouths. Within fifteen minutes, they each had wolfed down half a dozen cans of sardines and two loaves of bread.

"Best energy—finest kind," his dad said, smacking his lips and pulling his soaked gloves back on. Karl slipped his work gloves on and bent over the half-filled bait barrel. The stink of herring swirling in a brown muddy swill did nothing to upset his stomach. He'd baited traps for his dad since he was eight.

Overhead, the gulls screeched as he tossed them a handful of herring. They swooped low, scooping them off the top of waves, and angrily snapping at each other.

His dad smiled as he hooked a red and yellow buoy, slipped the rope over the hoist, took a turn or two on the winch, and hauled in a trap to the surface. Black-shelled lobsters thrashed about as water gushed out of the trap. Seth Bunker quickly uncoiled the twine holding the trap door, then pulled out a lobster and slipped it into the keep drum. He measured two more lobsters with a brass measure, tossed one back in the water, and thrust the other under the canvas of the keep drum.

Karl cleaned out kelp and seaweed, secured the bait bag, and closed and tied the trap door as his dad maneuvered the boat back into his string, and dropping the trap overboard.

They hadn't said much except to remark on the short-un's, trap cutters, and buoy cutters, and his dad commented on 'them darn summer people in their big boats, cutting lines.'

Around three o'clock, Karl took the wheel as they headed back to Mollusk Point Lighthouse and Quarry Cove while his dad swabbed the deck with a mop and flushed the gunwales with a bucket of water.

The gulls screeched, banking and screaming over the stern calling for a herring. His dad reached in the barrel and tossed a handful of syrupy herring waste overboard, then went back to flushing down the boat with a hose.

They were almost on Mollusk Point when his dad leaned up against the cuddy.

"Who do ya s'pose pulled the cork?"

"On the *Clamshell*?…dunno," Karl said. "Think somebody pulled it out?"

"How else," Seth Bunker said, pulling his fingers out of his gloves, and clapping them around the exhaust where they gave off a sizzle and steam.

"Unless we've got some gulls upset 'cause we didn't feed 'em—then, I don't think they have the knack of unscrewing brass caps, eh?"

"It does seem kind of strange, come to think of it. I couldn't have knocked it out…oh, I dunno, maybe just some kids playing around."

"Someone has it in for you. No kids around the cove would do that."

Seth Bunker stared straight ahead.

"I don't like it...don't like it one bit...no sir, not one bit."

Karl drew back on the throttle and quickly looked at his dad. "Whadya' mean, dad?"

Seth Bunker's brow tightened into a scowl, deep furrows lined his forehead. "Anyone who'd do a thing like that don't like you. Better stay on your toes. Anyone do something like that is capable of doing something even more dangerous."

It had to be Tripper, Karl knew, even though he didn't want to say it. It had to be, but Karl was not yet able to accept it. Then again...he thought.

"You keep your eyes peeled, and I'll be watching out for you, too," Seth Bunker said with a wink, slapping his son on his shoulder.

The *Laura* rubbed up against Phippen's Bait & Lobster Pound in Fisher Point, not far from the cove. Seth Bunker dropped a couple of half hitches around a dock piling. Together they hoisted the catch next to the scales by one of several keep holds in the large float. Wes Phippen, a heavy-set man with a boyish face, weighed the catch, then the barrel, and gave Karl a slip with the weight penciled on it.

"You sailing Saturday?" Wes asked, as Karl's dad climbed the walkway that rose and fell in the wake of the boats. "Hey, and what about them whales—they still thar?"

Karl's dad halted and turned. "Yeah, but not fer—"

"Hear they thinkin' o' harpooning 'em, eh?" Wes went on, as he busily weighed other catches and lobstermen collected their slips and walked up the gang plank to the office to get paid.

"Well, they ain't goin' to," Karl said, sternly looking at Wes. "We're going to get them back out to sea, soon as we can."

"Goin' ta be a lotta trouble, ain't there?" Wes said, shaking his big shoulders and flicking his nose. "Hear Nettie Beal might lose her house, and the cops picked her up for threatening to kill ol' Larry—gawd, that almost cracked me up, that did."

"We're going to get 'em back out to sea—wanna help us?"

"Sure, why not?" Wes Phippen said. "Foinest koind."

Wes untied the boat as Karl's dad backed away from the float, and turned and headed for Mollusk Point.

"See ya tomorrow," Wes called, as Karl waved back giving him a thumbs up. Karl's dad walked back, his arm extended, and slipped a twenty-dollar bill into Karl's hand.

Thursday was yet another pleasant day for hauling with another generous twenty-dollar bill reward to cap the day. For some reason, Seth Bunker seemed happier than ever. Perhaps it's having me along again, Karl thought. He was surprised his dad never mentioned the whales all day. He thought that strange, but thought his dad was skirting the issue to avoid arguments. But he did say something again that surprised Karl.

"Have you any idea who tried to scuttle the *Clamshell*?" he asked, as the *Laura* bobbed through swells back to Quarry Cove. "I don't like it when people start doing things like that. We're a pretty close community…always have been, that's why we don't have to lock the car and house doors."

"I haven't given it much thought…she was alright this morning," Karl said.

"Well, I must be getting old, but it sure bothers me. We just don't do that kind of stuff around here, and you know it."

As Karl rowed the skiff back to shore, he saw his dad's eyes focused on him.

"Don't you worry. I'm keeping a lookout for anything suspicious. I think it's all because of these whales. Meanwhile, you going to have a good sail on Saturday."

"Hope to, dad." We're going to be doing some planning tonight at Net'…Well, yeah, at Nettie's." His dad looked straight at him and chuckled.

After supper, Karl met Christine as she pedaled across 1A and onto the metal bridge that crossed the pool into Quarry

Cove. They swapped the day's events, as they leaned over the bridge and watched the two silent whales barely hidden below the surface of the pond. Crowds awaited higher tide for the evening show to begin, but Karl and Christine rode off to the lighthouse, gravel dust swirling around their bikes.

They talked until exhausted, trying to come up with some quick solution. But at nine o'clock they had just about given up. The whales were still in the pool and were likely to remain there, unless someone could find an answer before the regatta on Saturday.

Silently they rode home. Everything seemed hopeless. But as they stared across the handlebars of their bikes Christine broke into one of her famous mischievous grins.

"We still have Friday. Make some calls. I will too. Let's find out what the rest of the crew think. Then we'll have a war meeting at Nettie's and get ready for battle." She playfully punched Karl's arm, leaned across the bike handles. "Kiss me you fool," she said.

They kissed.

"You sound more like Bacall every time you do that," he chuckled.

"Then act like Bogey. Let's get tough." She swung her bike around and shot off across the metal bridge, waving as she crossed 1A and rounding the bend toward Pepper Mill and home.

22

The Plot Thickens

A surprised Karl answered the knock on the kitchen door after supper on Friday and stared into Christine's face.

"Come on, you've got to come," she said, reaching for Karl's arm as his dad paused and muttered a greeting to her, and then walked into the parlor and turned on the radio.

"Come on in, Christine," Karl's mom said, walking to the door. Christine nervously shook her head, smiling, and glancing in the general direction of the parlor.

"Oh, he won't bother you," Karl's mom said, reaching for Christine's arm.

"We have to go," Christine said, drawing back. "It's an emergency…a real emergency." She gripped Karl's arm pulling him across the doorstep.

"Hold on…I haven't got my shoes on," he said, slipping into his sneakers.

He flipped his leg over his Schwinn and raced behind her as she coasted down Quarry Cove Hill toward the bridge. The tide was rising, and a growing crowd of people was filling up the 1A parking lot. Strains of *Yankee Doodle* floated across the cove from Johnny's lunch wagon. A state trooper's cruiser was parked alongside the highway and the police cruiser faced the pool, with Joe Mullins slouched against the driver's door with smoke curling from the cigarette pinched between his fingers.

"What's going on?" he called out, as Christine thrust out her left leg, sending up a cloud of dust and gravel as she cut left onto the causeway.

"Can't tell ya 'til we get to Nettie's," Christine called back.

She was up the steps and onto the porch, then inside the kitchen as Karl stumbled after her.

"It's happened," Nettie started. "This Saturday is the day," she said, her fists clenched as she walked stiffly between the sink and the table. "They're going to do it." She pounded the table with her fist.

Karl stared vacantly at Christine. "Do what?" he asked incredulously.

"They're going to...they're going to kill the whales." Nettie swung around, her face taut.

Christine jumped up, staring unbelieving at Nettie, who leaned on the kitchen table with her face drawn tight and her eyes burning with anger.

"But they're not going to," she said, knotting her fists. "And you know what?" she said, staring at Karl who looked blank. "I wonder if your dad is working with Chief Harrington?"

"He's not all that keen on Woody," Karl said. "But I just spent two days lobsterin' with him and he never said anything," Karl said. "So that's why...that's why he was so nice to me."

Nettie and Christine exchanged puzzled looks and looked back at Karl.

"But...wait. He even waited for me while I bailed out my boat...it was ready to sink. He even gave me twenty bucks yesterday and another twenty today. He knew all the time," he said, slumping over in his chair. Then, smacking his fist into his palm, he looked at Christine and Nettie who just stared blankly at him. "Sure, no wonder he was all for the regatta with no problem about me being in it. Once we're out of the way... How could he do such a thing? He wants me out of the way with the rest of the kids tomorrow, and then they'll do it...whatever it is they plan to do."

"Right. When you're out sailing, he and the Chief and that Joe Mullins are planning to get rid of the whales," Nettie said. "I wouldn't have known had it not been for Joe, but don't say anything. The Chief's behind the whole thing."

"What can we do?" Christine said, looking at Nettie and Karl. "We've got to do something...but what?"

Nettie was on the phone talking to Malcolm Hadlock at WBCF in Portland with a scoop. Then she called WBAN in Bangor. Frustrated, she shook her head and pounded her fist on the table. Hopelessly she stared at the ceiling.

"Look, I don't know exactly what's going to happen. But I can tell you something will happen. So you'd better get your reporters up here – or miss the story of the year. Something very big is about to happen," she added.

"I don't believe it. What do I have to do to convince them?" she said, throwing her arms askew and plodding across the kitchen floor.

"But will they come?" Christine anxiously asked, catching up to Nettie.

"What have you got to do to convince them?" Karl asked.

Nettie spun around. "Do? – I did it. I think I've got them. Then she flung her arms around Karl's and Christine's shoulders and happily walked back to the table. "One more thing," she said briskly walking back to the telephone.

She didn't have so much trouble convincing the newspapers. She called the Sunday paper, the weekly, and the dailies. Digging through the yellow pages, she dug up the Associated Press and United Press bureaus and called them in Portland.

"That's good," she said beaming as she hung up. "The AP and UP are calling their stringers and getting them on it – whoo…oo!"

23

Grand Strategy

Karl and Christine excitedly looked at each other. "If the press shows up, they're going to have a hard time carrying out their plans," Christine said.

"But what if they don't?" It was like Karl had dropped a stone down a well as all three waited expectantly for the splash.

"They will. They have to," Christine finally broke the silence as Nettie's brow furrowed with worry as she banged her fists together.

"There's no guarantee," Karl said, as both women stared blankly at him. "They usually like to report after its happened – not before. Besides, they've been broadcasting and reporting on the whales all week. It's old news."

"That's right. You're right," Nettie said. "I had a tough time trying to convince them. We have to do something – something drastic – as drastic as what the chief and his big white hunters are planning." She quickly walked up and down the kitchen, her doubled fist tapping her lips. Christine just sat at the table, head bent, attempting to conjure up a plan.

"I got it." It was Karl. Christine looked up. Nettie stopped pacing. Both stared hard at Karl who beckoned them to the table.

"Tarzan," he said, his face beaming. The women looked blankly at each other.

"What-at?" Christine asked, her hands dropping into her lap. "Are you alright?"

"Don't knock it. We sure could use Tarzan right about now," Nettie said with a hearty chuckle. "You got his number?" Christine burst out laughing. But Karl was unperturbed.

"I was just thinking about how Tarzan saved the elephants and managed to hide them from the great white hunters."

A wide smile flashed across Christine's face. Nettie rushed to the table, her face beaming and her fists tight.

"We can do the same thing," Karl said excitedly.

"But how?" Christine said, a puzzled look stretched across her face.

"I think he's got it," Nettie said excitedly. "I think I know what he's got," she said. "Go on…go on."

"The regatta," Karl said, his face a triumphant glow. Then he rose quickly from the table. Nettie and Christine followed him as she walked, head down, hands clasped, muttering. Then he stopped. "Yes…yes…yes," he said spinning around.

He scrambled into a chair again at the table and stared hard at Christine and Nettie.

"We're going to have to do some running and phoning tonight to get a hold of those in the regatta," he said. "I bet there isn't one participant who won't help," Karl said, banging his fist victoriously on the table.

"We're going to rob the hunters of their prey," he said, smacking a fist into his other palm.

Three heads were almost pressed together across the kitchen table, as Karl quickly sketched out his plan. Both women listened intently, then leaned back and delightedly clapped their hands. "It's a simple plan," he said, "and I bet we can carry it out if Christine can get her dad to help…and, yes, you, Nettie. Get your Coast Guard son to help us. When he had finished, Karl beamed as Christine and Nettie hugged him, planting kisses on his cheeks.

Nettie was busy dialing as she faced the wall. She laughed in between conversations, as Christine firmly gripped Karl's arm.

"Hello, Darlin'," she started, winking at Christine and Karl.

"Marvelous," Nettie said, after a fifteen-minute chat. Hanging up the receiver, she faced the happy kids. "That didn't take long…he's a good kid, just like his dad. They'll be here."

"Now it's up to your dad, Christine," Karl said.

"He'll help. I know he will…but—wait a minute…"

Nettie and Karl waited apprehensively.

"His boat…I mean…he was having problems…let's hope he's got it going again."

"He'd better," Karl said, "Or else we're doomed."

Christine called home and rattled away with her dad, shaking her head as her expression changed from joy to desperation…

"It's fifty-fifty," she said, finally putting the phone down, "but, guess what?"

Karl and Nettie looked at her hopefully.

"If his won't go, he says he'll get one that will."

The threesome let out a cheer.

Between Nettie's phone calls and Christine and Karl's house visits throughout Quarry Cove and Pepper Mill Cove, nearly all of the regatta sailors were contacted, except for Jilly Hanes and Tom Clark, who'd gone to the movies in Camden.

It was eleven o'clock when two spirited and happy young people kissed goodnight. Karl Bunker and Christine Alley then mounted their bikes and pedaled back to Quarry Cove and Pepper Mill village under a full moon. Only a trace of dust trailed them as the tires on their bikes crunched and crackled along the gravelly Mollusk Point causeway.

24

Foiling the Plot

Saturday was a picture-perfect calendar day for a regatta. Gentle breezes rippled across Quarry Cove. Lobster boats tugged at moorings, and dinghies rubbed quietly against the slips. Karl lost little time donning his khaki trousers, white socks, sneakers, and a sweater. His spoon scraped a few spoonsful of cereal into his mouth and then he was off.

"No good eating that way," his mom said. "And, here— what's going on?" she said, catching his forearm. "Your dad was on the phone for a long time last night. What was that all about?"

"Don't know about dad, all I know is that today is the annual Quarry Cove and Pepper Mill Regatta," he said sliding past her and opening the kitchen door.

"Yes, and there's something else, isn't there?" his mother persisted.

He stepped back in the kitchen, kissed her on the cheek and was on his bike before his father had time to catch him as he sailed down Cove Hill.

Main sails and jibs flapped and tugged at rigging from some masts in the cove, with sailors from Pepper Mill sailing past Mollusk Point lighthouse, and others puttering into the assembly area by Spooner's Wharf, their dinghies pushed by small sputtering eggbeater motors.

Some drew their boats up on shore, while the others tied up at several slips on either side of the cove, waving and calling out to each other.

Chauncey Philpot made his official arrival all spruced up in his pin-striped suit. A light brown baseball cap covered his bald pate, and sat on his bushy sideburns. Brand new white and blue sneakers stuck their toes out below his trouser cuffs.

"Well, well, well," he started, "what a wonder, wonderful day." Some of the kids smirked or shook their heads, chuckling. "We are going to have a wonderful race today, aren't we?" he said to no one in particular, though many nodded and agreed.

Chauncey carefully flipped the legal size pages on his clipboard with the names of the contestants, his eyes widening, his face beaming.

"It's a big field...more than I've ever seen," he said.

"How many?" Karl asked, anxiously as he stepped side to side around people, and standing on his toes, searched up and down the shoreline for Christine.

Chauncey ran his pencil over the sheets counting quietly.

A gorilla-sized hand clasped Karl's shoulder and he looked up into the round, smiling red face of Tiny Stinson. "We're here, buddy," he said, giving him a friendly tap on his shoulder, "and we're ready to go to work."

Within fifteen minutes the cove was a flash of colorful white sails, some dabbed with logos—a flash of red lightning, blue anchors, a wild-looking pirate with a black eye patch. The two-horsepower eggbeaters puttered as contestants swarmed around the dock, yelling to each other, and laughing and waving. Perched on a large square lobster keep box sat Chauncey Philpot, taking in the grand scene.

"I've never seen such a crowd...what a crowd...my word."

Karl followed the boats and stopped as one passed in front of his father's lobster boat. He pulled at the buoy as the wake of the boats churned the pool.

They're all here, Karl thought, shifting his eyes back to the bridge and the parking lot.

The crowd swelled around the bridge. He could just make out Joe Mullins, standing by his police cruiser, the smoke trailing out of his nose and mouth, and a state trooper waving traffic along on 1A. His face tightened as he saw Tripper Gleason slumped on the hood of his dad's Cadillac. The Greenfields were also there. Larry sat huddled over the steering wheel, and Belinda and Darrell were perched on the sides of the truck. He was sure Darrell was holding a harpoon. Then he tensed even more as Chief Harrington was desperately trying to get people to leave the bridge. Joe Mullins stood at the end of the bridge encouraging the people to keep moving.

Karl felt it hard to believe that his dad would go along with something like this. Fear knotted his stomach. He scanned the bridge, the pathway by the shore, and the parking lot across the cove.

"Fifty-five," Chauncey Philpot coughed, as if to accentuate the number.

Karl turned to face Chauncey.

"It's got to be a record," Chauncey said, his face beaming.

Karl nodded in agreement. Excited cheers and shouts rose above the pool. His spirits soared. The chief may have harpoon hunters and "tripper" Gleason and his rifle, but he felt a surging confidence rising within him as the cheering dinghy crews got even louder.

"We're going to show 'em...we'll show 'em," they shouted.

"Sorry, I missed that," Chauncey said, happily cupping his hand to his ear. "It's so noisy. Everyone's in such good spirits."

Chauncey put aside the tablet and started printing large black numbers on white cards. For a while Karl watched as Chauncey drew large numbers on the white card in his meticulous penmanship.

"Looks like you printed them," Karl said, as Chauncey looked somewhat dubiously at him. "I mean, like you had them printed."

Chauncey smiled and nodded his appreciation.

The plan of action hadn't been written down. But after several hours of calling and knocking on doors, which concluded just a few hours ago, it was now the prime mission of all of the young participants.

The worry or fear that had plagued Karl had gone. He was now buoyed by the spirit and enthusiasm of the sailors. This year, the regatta would take second place as they all vowed that their only goal that day would be to save the whales. But despite all of his confidence, he knew the big job lay ahead. They had to move and move fast.

But where was Christine? Karl walked to the head of the dock, now surrounded by more and more sailing dinghies and kids shouting and waving. He shielded his eyes against a glaring white sun which painted the foam whiter, and dappled the shoreline as it filtered through the pine and birch.

The crowd was getting bigger. But it was not so much for the regatta as it was for the morning show by Bustah and Bumpah. The ripples were widening the pool. And two large round orange lumps could be seen just below the muddy surface. *Yankee Doodle Dandy* flavored the air, a fair breeze capturing segments and spilling them across the cove. A ring of flags strained at their short staffs over Johnny's lunch wagon.

They had to move—and move fast.

"Karl, Karl!"

A toot on her father's air horn followed her calls. Karl reached down and caught the line her dad tossed him, as he guided his boat alongside the dock and cut the engine.

Karl dropped a couple of half hitches over a dock piling, reached for her hand and pulled her onto the slip. She looked sharp in her sailing rig, tan slacks, sneakers and a white sweater with 'P & Q Regatta' embroidered over the left pocket. Her fragrance numbed his mind. Her loving peck on the cheek sent chills through his body.

"I thought you'd never make it," he said, turning and pulling her along.

"I was talking with Nettie," Christine said, pointing across the pool where Nettie was, waving madly and blowing kisses, one hand clutching her sign. Karl waved back, and clambered up the crawl walk with her dad in tow.

"Now, listen," her dad said. "I want both of you be real careful, and be sure to take good care of her, Karl." He reached

117

out, drawing their hands together in a warm clasp of a mutual pledge. "Now, let's get this little problem solved. Is your dad there?"

Surprised, Karl looked at Christine's dad and back at the bridge. "He's there," he said pointing to where his dad was standing next to the chief.

Karl raised his hands, puzzled. "Good luck," he said, smiling, as he turned and briskly strode off toward the bridge.

"Why did he want to know about my dad?" Karl said "I thought they were ready to go at it at the meeting."

"Not my dad. He always believes there's another way," Christine said, seeing his perplexed look and hugging his arm. "Don't worry – you'll see."

Chauncey Philpot grinned and bid them luck as he handed them the number "21." They skipped together down the gangplank, and climbed aboard the *Clamshell*. They stuck the cardboard between the gunwale slats and unreefed the mainsail, as Christine hauled it to the head of the mast.

"We'll keep the motor on, just in case," Karl said, as Christine ran the jib up and knotted the jib sheets.

"Way to go, Karl," Eric Beal shouted to him. Many of his fellow mariners raised their fists with a determined cheer.

"Come on, let's do it," a happy Christine shouted above the noise.

There was a roar as the mariners cheered, thumped their fists in the air and revved up their motors. A long white rope of waving sail tied to masts of fifty-five dinghies moved slowly and determinedly toward the bridge with Karl and Christine leading the flotilla.

Karl stood up. "Let's go," he shouted, his voice almost breaking. Fifty-five captains and fifty-five mates cheered, their eggbeaters straining.

Chauncey Philpot's right fist, clenching the starting pistol, thrust it high above his shoulders. His voice crackled through the megaphone.

"Are you ready?"

There was a pop followed by a puff of white smoke darting from his pistol. He shook a little and hastily sat down. But he was barely seated, when he leapt back on his feet. Scrambling through a pile of papers on the table he grabbed the megaphone. Excitedly he clicked and re-clicked the mike button, which mangled his message and voice.

"No, no, no," he yelled. The mike finally responded. "Not that way! The other way!"

Frantically, he jabbed his index finger across his nose, pointing to the sea.

"Now hear this..." he started with the best growl he could muster. It was like that in all Navy movies. "Now hear this..." but the long line of boats, getting longer and longer just kept cruising toward the bridge.

Exasperated, Chauncey stood transfixed, his jaw dropped. The youngsters passing by good naturedly waved to him.

"Don't go away, Chauncey, we'll be back," one yelled to him. His crew mate blew him a kiss. Chauncey embarrassedly shook his hands, his whole body trembling.

"But, but, but..." Chauncey exclaimed. No one heard him. The outboards were almost screaming as the flotilla "putt-putt-puttered" toward the bridge with Karl and Christine leading in Dinghy 21.

But with all of the noise, the flap of sail, masts groaning and squeaking, and the buzz of motors, a sudden hush settled across the pool. The crowd came to see the whales. But a big white shroud was being drawn across the pool, and they couldn't see anything. Disappointedly, they picked up what others were doing, and like Chauncey, erratically pointed to the sea.

Christine hauled the tiller over and started a wide sweep around the pool by the bridge and around the bubbles popping on the surface. Karl caught the handle of the bait bucket and waddled amidships as Christine braced. Her face puckered as

Karl tore the cover off the bucket holding a week-long old batch of herring.

"Steady as she goes," she cried out, "or you'll be eating herring."

"You're okay," Karl said, settling into the cockpit, and jerking his head up at the bridge.

An angry Chief Harrington stood stiffly by the railing glaring down at Christine and Karl.

"What's this all about…you're going the wrong way," he called out.

"Hi, Chief," Karl shouted back. Christine waved briefly taking her eyes off the two rings of bubbles which were growing wider and wider.

"Boy, does he ever look happy," Christine said with a chuckle. "And look at your pal Tripper…he's almost coming apart – poor baby." Karl glanced up at the railing where Tripper glared down at them.

"Get an eyeful, Tripper," Karl said. "A good one, 'cause it'll be the last you ever see of these whales." Reaching into the bucket he cupped a handful of herring and dunked it in the pool.

The waters parted and two huge snouts rose. Two pairs of eyes quickly took in the scene before their noses picked up the scent and they nosed underwater with a terrific splash which sent dinghies bouncing as if hit by a tidal wave.

Karl scooped more fish out of the bucket as a large snout popped up next to his hand. Quickly he dropped the fish and drew back as the other whale came in for a feed.

"They're coming," Christine said excitedly. "They're taking the bait." She gunned the engine a little as Karl dipped more fish. Both whales were now alongside the dinghy. "This is fantastic," Christine shouted. "Just look at them…keep feeding them."

Twenty-one was now the point dinghy. And, as planned, the other dinghies swung into a large protective loop behind Karl and Christine. The whales were now encircled and staying close behind Twenty-One which was leading the flotilla.

People started to shout, upset that their vision of the whales was being blocked.

A frustrated Chief Harrington ran to the center of the bridge. Leaning over the railing, he angrily shouted at the young mariners "Get out…go on, get out, we've got work to do."

A roar of uncomplimentary comments sallied back to the shocked chief, who just stood and stared in disbelief.

"I'll never believe this," Christine said as a whopping cheer went up from the Pepper Mill side of the cove.

She and Karl stared as a forest of white signs started to wave back and fro, accompanied by a chorus of adults and children chanting "Save the whales…Save the whales…"

Bustah and Bumpah surfaced and somersaulted. Karl and Christine exchanged anxious glances.

"They've gone," Christine said. "Quickly – throw some more fish for them."

"They're just showing off," Karl said. "They'll be back for a curtain call."

Two snouts immediately popped to the surface, and Karl scooped up a handful of the dripping fish and dropped them in the water. There was a swirl of water as two large and two small flippers broke the surface and quickly disappeared. Dinghies heaved in the swell left by the whales. Barely a second elapsed and a large snout with two tiny eyes behind it popped up and smiled at Christine, showing off all of its bright white teeth.

There was a low hum, a whistle, and a "clickety-click" as Bumpah joined in.

Karl wasted little time thrusting his hand back into the barrel as Christine held her sleeve against her nose. Bumpah came nearer to the side of the boat as Karl flung out the herring and both whales dove as the crowd roared with approval on the beach.

Gently, Christine eased the motor's accelerator slightly forward again as both sails flapped, unfettered.

"They must be really ripped off," Christine said, as she looked at the crowd and saw Chief Harrison walking with a concerned air along the bridge rail. "This is fantastic."

Bustah and Bumpah surfaced again, and gently rubbed up against the *Clamshell* as Christine steadied herself against the transom.

"Quick—feed them!" she said with a laugh, as the whales pushed their snouts against the side of the dinghy. Karl flung another handful of herring overboard and the whales dove again and the crowd roared.

Back on the bridge an angrier chief watched disgustedly as the sailboats lassoed the whales and drew the noose into a narrow circle. The crowd started to cross the bridge to see more clearly.

"Get back. You can't come on here," he shouted. But the crowd inched closer to the center of the bridge where the chief stood.

"We want to see the whales," a small girl cried out.

"Why are you stopping us from seeing the whales?" an upset mother added.

"Madam...it's not my fault. These kids...these sailors, or whatever...Well, yes. They're taking them out to sea."

"Why?" asked a man. "Yes. There's no need to do that...is there?" another man asked.

"Only if someone wants to shoot them," the angry voice of Nettie cried.

The crowd turned to face her. Then they peppered the chief with questions.

"You mean you're going to stand here while people shoot the whales," an angry tourist demanded as the chief gulped.

He glared as the other boats formed a circle around the whales. Karl and Christine's dinghy was at the head of the group, gradually easing out of the pool toward the lighthouse and open sea. Christine held the tiller in one hand.

"As long as we don't run out of fish, we'll have the whales," Karl said, dipping his hand into the bucket and dropping a handful of oily and slippery fish into the water, as the whales bobbed to the surface briefly and dived down to get the fish. Slowly 21's put-put clawed its way toward the lighthouse, the whales' flukes cutting through a choppy channel.

Karl twisted around. There was a commotion on the bridge. Amid the angry shouts and crying children, and Nettie waving her sign, he caught sight of the Greenfields running across the bridge with their harpoons and bows and arrows. Right behind them strode Tripper, his rifle across his chest, ready to start shooting.

"You kids had better leave the pool." It was the creaky, mechanical megaphone voice of Chief Harrington speaking as he leaned over the bridge railing. "You kids are being ordered to leave the pool," he barked out again.

"We are," one of the boaters cried back.

"I don't believe this," Christine said, pointing to the Greenfields and Tripper, who defiantly jammed a round into his rifle and pulled the bolt back. "Oh, no," she cried out. "Look —he's aiming at us!"

"This is Chief Harrington. You are hereby ordered to leave the pool, or—"

His voice stopped, and a babble of angry and tinny voices could be heard in the background over the open mike.

"We'd better move out," Karl said, as Christine gave the motor another notch of power, and watching as Bustah and Bumpah stalked 21, a large fluke and smaller fluke barely moving, but powerfully thrusting the whales forward.

Men and women were shouting on the bridge. They both looked up to see Tiny holding Tripper's rifle, and two more men chasing the Greenfields off the bridge. A loud yell went up from the sign wavers who started to march across the bridge with Nettie leading the throng.

"Did you see that?" Christine said, staring unbelievably at the bridge, as Karl kept tossing herring to the whales.

Not far behind, the wide circle of boats had now tightened into a "U" surrounding the whales behind the *Clamshell*. Periodically they would dive then surface and shoot a small fountain of water out of their blowholes.

"That Tiny...he's one great guy," Karl said.

"Sure is...but did you see who was chasing the Greenfields?"

"Too busy feeding these monsters," Karl said, happily dropping a handful of herring into the water, as thin, brown watery juice dripped from his fingers.

"Look," she said, pointing to the crowded parking lot as two men hustled the Greenfields into their pickup and tossed the bows and arrows into the back.

"Is that your dad?" Karl said. "Oh my gawd...look who's with him!"

Christine shuffled close to him, her right arm under her nose.

"It's my dad! I don't believe it," he said, shaking his head. "I just don't believe it."

She gripped his arm and quickly covered her nose again. "Phew. How much more of that horrid stuff do you have? – What a stink!"

"Lobsters eat it – but nobody complains," he shouted back.

A cloud of brown dust spiraled up over the parking lot and a black Cadillac threw up gravel and brown dust as it tore into Route 1A with Tiny running after it waving his hambone fist.

"Got rid of him," Karl said gleefully, and glanced up at the bridge falling astern as the *Clamshell* puttered and gurgled toward Mollusk Point lighthouse.

For a second or so he stopped ladling the herring and stared at the small group of people still surrounding the chief. Angry sign wavers pushed and waved their signs under the chief's nose, as they furiously berated the chief. Two stocky men suddenly pushed through the sign wavers and angrily started wagging their fingers ion the chief's face. The chief looked shocked and hopeless. His right hand man, Mullins was casually strolling along the bridge, dragging on a cigarette.

For an instant, Karl just sat and stared unable to believe that a riot was taking place on the bridge. He had never seen anything like this in Quarry Cove.

"Karl? Quick!" It was Christine frantically waving her free hand and pointing at the two whales that had suddenly turned and were ready to go under the loop formed by the dinghies. Quickly he scooped up a load of dripping herring and tossed it into the water, calling like he was trying to entice a cat.

"Here…kitty, kitty…I mean...Bustah and Bumpah. Then he started to mimic Nettie's "Coolah, cool, tsk, tsk, tsk…" The whales spun around. Christine laughed and the *Clamshell* headed toward the shore.

"Keep feeding them," she said. "Don't let up or we'll lose them."

"Stay on course, or we'll lose this boat – too." Frantically he dipped herring and flung them at the two whales that apparently quickly picked up the scent and sliced through the water to the *Clamshell*.

"A bit more gas," Karl said, anxiously baiting and trying to follow the action on the bridge. The loop formed by the other dinghies tightened and the whales seemed more interested in eating than noticing that they were being enticed out to sea.

As Karl and Christine passed a confused Chauncey Philpot they both waved. Chauncey seemed relieved. Picking up his megaphone, he waved back and wished them good luck through the tinny speaker.

"You're being followed," Chauncey's voice crackled over the megaphone, as he pointed excitedly toward the whales directly behind the *Clamshell*. Karl and Christine waved back.

"Almost out of here," Christine shouted, "almost."

Up ahead the peppermint-striped Mollusk Point Lighthouse loomed tall, dominating the entrance to Quarry Cove. An excited Christine clenched her hands up to her face and let out a "Wow."

"Almost," Karl shouted back above the hum of the fleet's motors and crash and wash of waves on the rocks surrounding Mollusk Point.

The Rush to the Sea

Just off Mollusk Point Lighthouse, Christine trimmed the mainsail and Karl adjusted the jib. A southwesterly breeze as the *Clamshell* filled the sails on a starboard tack. Cutting the motor, Christine snapped her finger toward giant red buoy Number 4, swaying slowly in the chop, its big bell gonging like a lonely monastery on a Tibetan hill.

"Yeah – we did it." Her sharp cry was picked up by the rest of the boats, as Karl steadied himself amidships from the shock. Others yelled and waved their arms victoriously.

All the boats had cleared Mollusk Point. The loop had now fanned out into a line as boat crews cut their motors and trimmed sail. The wind was picking up and the boats spread out drawing a wide V behind the *Clamshell* which formed a giant catch net behind the whales.

"We're on our way," Karl said, as the dinghy's bow rose and slapped the swell. "We don't have far to go," he said, as Christine steered toward the channel between pine-crested Black Isle and Hawk Island, shores carpeted in rough red rock.

Bumpah and Bustah slid silently behind the *Clamshell* like two small submarines. Karl took the plastic bucket and poured some of the brownish water over the gunwale.

"Just to make sure they're still with us," he said.

A big patch of white sail carpeted the sea as the flotilla spread out behind the *Clamshell*. Red, yellow and blue telltales streamed almost straight out inside the sails. The wind was picking up and the boats were getting an extra surge through the waves.

No one was keeping track of time, but it must have been thirty minutes or more that the *Clamshell* in the lead with Bustah and Bumpah in tow, was clear of The Narrows.

"So far, so good," Karl said, his right continuously dipping and serving the whales a herring treat. "These guys won't be able to eat for a week," he said as Bustah and Bumpah showed off their snouts.

"They look very happy," Christine shouted. "I think Bustah just winked at me."

"That's something. How'd ya know who's who?"

"Easy. The big one is Bustah. Bumpah must be his brother," Christine said, as the dinghy swayed amid the chop.

"Everything's going swell," Karl said, as Christine held the tiller and main sheet. "Let's hope your dad meets us."

"Karl, look!" Christine's arm shot out west of the lighthouse. With its bow riding high atop the waves, a thirty-four-foot lobster boat cut through the chop directly toward the *Clamshell*.

"Son of a gun – that's Tripper," Karl said, "and he's coming right for us."

Tripper was behind the helm. Next to him, Karl made out the Greenfield kids, all staring hard through the windshield.

"They don't give up," Karl said. "Keep her going straight ahead," he said, as he tightened the jib as the *Clamshell* surged along.

Karl was horrified to see Greenfield take the wheel from Tripper who moved off to the side of the boat. "Stay low," he hissed to Christine, as Tripper snapped the bolt back on his rifle and began to sight in.

An angered Christine stood up, feet apart bracing against chop. "Have you gone mad? Put that rifle down and don't be so idiotic!" she screamed. The rest of the flotilla saw what was happening and a huge roar rose above the water with boys and girls shouting and waving their fists at the boat which continued to bear down on the *Clamshell*.

"Jeez...don't let go of the helm," Karl shouted diving toward the stern past Christine and grabbing the helm. "He's out of his freaking mind," Karl shouted. "Stupid? He's gone bats." He braced himself and frantically waved at Gleason, now sighting in on the whales.

"You've gone nuts, you crazy bastard?" he shouted, his voice lost in the roar of Tripper's dad's boat.

"Watch out, Karl...he's going to shoot you," Christine shouted.

Tripper suddenly lowered the rifle and jabbed his fingers toward the stern of the *Clamshell* yelling at the Greenfields to steer toward the *Clamshell*. Once again he raised his rifle and swept the barrel along the hull of the *Clamshell,* stopping at the stern where the two whales' flukes moved effortlessly.

"You'd better drop that rifle, Tripper, or I'll flatten you," Karl shouted.

"You are the stupidest piece of crap I've ever seen," Christine screamed, waving her fist at him.

But the high school football star and teacher's pet seemed delighted by the attention. He brought the rifle up to his shoulder, to sight in again on the whales as his boat bobbed up and down.

"I could sink the lotta ya," he shouted, and fired a shot across the bow of Bob Roberts' twelve-foot *Titanic,* one of the boats in the flotilla. Roberts almost fell overboard as he jumped out of his seat and yelled at Tripper. The Greenfields were amidships fixing their arrows into the bows. Tripper scoffed at Roberts and raised his rifle again.

Tripper was still laughing, tracking his targets, when a half-dozen dinghies drew a white curtain of canvas between his boat and the *Clamshell*, their angry crews waving fists and yelling obscenities at Tripper and the Greenfields.

As the long white sail curtain sailed past the boat, Tripper slowly lowered his rifle and stared across the reach as a Coast

Guard cutter sliced through the seas, its prow clean out of the water.

A blast from the cutter's horn bounced and echoed across the bay. Then another blast, and yet another. Within minutes, it was less than a thousand yards away, still blowing its horn.

Tripper and the Greenfields disappeared under the cuddy. The engine gurgled, blowing out a black smoke balloon, and one of the Greenfields started to swing the bow away from the scene, just as a deep stern voice crackled across the water.

"This is the U.S Coast Guard. You, in the lobster boat, heave to. Stay where you are. Repeat. Do not get underway. Stay where you are, and prepare for boarding."

A loud cheer arose from amid the sails of the dinghy fleet as Tripper's boat rocked back and forth, the engine in neutral. The cutter's engines had been throttled back as the skipper eased past the head of the dinghy fleet and drew alongside Tripper's boat.

Hurriedly, Tripper ran to the stern and dropped something overboard.

Christine hugged Karl and kissed him. "See that?" Christine said. "He dumped his rifle."

The cutter rubbed up against the lobster boat and two armed crewmen from the Coast Guard lightly hopped over the gunwales. Tripper stood amidships his hands stretched above his head, as a crewman patted him down. Another came from under the cuddy with an armful of archery equipment and harpoons.

"I hope they lock him up—and that Greenfield trash," Christine said, watching the action.

Karl gave a nod of approval.

"Me, too. That guy has gone berserk. He's crazy like the rest of 'em."

The *Clamshell* and the rest of the dinghy fleet maintained their course, though Karl and Christine had a tough time concentrating on direction as they watched the cutter's Captain confront Tripper and his crew. The Greenfields and Tripper were waving their hands and arms pointing toward the flotilla as the

Coast Guard skipper had the trio standing amidships with their arms high above their heads.

"Wish I could hear what they are saying," Christine said. "That should shut them up — that's for sure. This is great though, isn't it?" she said excitedly shaking her hands.

"Sure is. But I still don't understand it," Karl said. "I just don't get it. I can't understand why that guy is so jealous."

"I don't know why he should be, I never encouraged him. We went to the movies once, and that was it, enough. But this kind of stuff is dangerous. Someone's going to get hurt."

Karl held onto the mast as he watched the confrontation aboard Tripper's dad's boat.

He'd almost forgotten Bustah and Bumpah, when the boat got a bump followed by a clicker-clack.

"Someone is getting hungry," Christine said with a chuckle. "Feed those whales."

An engine roared and the Gleason boat slowly pulled away from the cutter and headed back to port. The cutter held its position, the Coast Guard apparently watching Gleason's boat, and then swung around to the head of the dinghy fleet.

From atop the short bridge, the captain held his megaphone and called out to the fleet.

"Everyone, okay? We'll stay with you until you make contact with the *Laura.*

Karl gave him thumbs up and turned to Christine.

"Whadya make of that? Boy—that Nettie!" He shook his head and scooped up a handful of herring. "Did I hear him right? Did he say the *Laura?*"

"Dad's boat must have gone on the blink again," Christine said, "so they must be using your dad's."

"But how could that be?" Karl said, shaking his head, as he scooped the herring and dropped them overboard, the two whales eating them up.

131

The fleet sailed majestically in two lines through The Narrows, circled another big red buoy, and heaved to. Sails luffed as the sailors hooked onto each other's craft.

They all gave a big cheer as the Coast Guard cutter circled at the head of the fleet, gave a roaring toot and gently pulled away, the captain waving.

There was a big toot-toot and an answering salute as the *Laura* passed the cutter, steaming swiftly to the head of the dinghy fleet.

With a roar and a belch of black exhaust, the *Laura* swung her stern toward Karl and Christine's dinghy.

"We're a bit late, but we made it," a delighted Nettie cried out to them from the stern. "But I see my boy made it on time," she said nodding her head toward the departing cutter.

Christine swung the tiller, nudging the gunwale against the *Laura*'s stern.

Karl quickly reached down and picked up a pail of herring bait.

"Here…I can get it," a gruff voice said over the stern, as the man extended two hambone hands tethered to hairy arms.

Karl released the pail and almost toppled overboard.

Christine was speechless, too.

"Dad?" said Karl.

"Dad?" said Christine.

Smiles ringed their father's faces as they looked down from the stern.

"Isn't this great?" a delighted Nettie sang out amidships, running astern and wrapping her arms around both men.

"But—" Christine's voice broke.

"Everything's going to be just fine," her dad said. "Ain't it Seth?"

"But what happ—?" Christine started.

"Boat's on the blink again. It's okay…don't you worry," her father said, chuckling.

"Yeah, we'll get these Bumpah and Bustah fellas back out to where they belong. Don't you worry. Now, let's get the rest of that bait you pinched out of my boat, young man," Seth Bunker said, staring at his son. "It's alright. We had a good talk. So don't you worry."

"Isn't this great?" Nettie said. "Let's get going though so my darlings don't lose interest."

Seth Bunker raised his eyebrows, shook his head, and held back a grin.

Karl eased the boat away as another dinghy eased alongside of them. Christine clung to Karl as they watched their dads haul up another pail of bait.

The men hauled up four pails of bait from the dinghies, while Nettie whistled and clicked her tongue and tossed out herring heads and tails.

Leaning over the gunwale, pursing her lips, Nettie made a soft, mellow call.

"Oo-ooh-ooh."

"See. That's how you do it," Christine said, looping her arm around Karl's shoulders, as his dad rolled his head and eyes.

"Canaries of the sea," Nettie said.

"I'm no canary," Karl said.

"That's for sure," Christine chuckled. "I don't think you even whistle."

There was a big splash behind the *Clamshell* as Bustah and Bumpah dove under the dinghy and popped up behind the *Laura*.

Christine and Karl sat silently as the *Laura* spat and bubbled water out of the stern, then slowly, and almost noiselessly rumbled away with a contented chug-a-chug.

Nettie was leaning over the gunwale. With a bucket resting on the stern, she reached in and scooped a handful of herring and dropped it overboard. Then she laughed as two snouts popped up. Happily, she waved to Christine and Karl. Christine's dad and Karl's dad turned and gave a big wave.

"Bye Bustah. Bye Bumpah," Christine said sadly, her hand poised above her waist.

"You'd better head back, we've got some fog to contend with," Christine's dad called out.

"Moving up along the coast pretty darn fast, I'd say," Seth Bunker shouted.

"Not too fast, now dad," Nettie said, as the *Laura* inched away.

"Well," said Christine.

"Well," said Karl.

26

Mission Accomplished

Too shocked to say anything, Karl took the luff out of the mainsail and sprang forward to tend the jib, as Christine took the mainsail sheet and rudder.

The *Laura* chugged slowly toward Deer Isle Bridge, a rolling wash of foam and screaming seagulls in its wake, and a trail of smoke twirling above the cuddy. Nettie was waving and tossing fish heads into the wake, as the two white snouts kept popping to the surface, then rolling, and blowing streams of water.

Christine and Karl were still waving as the *Laura* steamed under the span and headed for the open sea.

Christine hugged Karl as the *Clamshell* rocked steadily in the swell.

"This is fantastic! I just can't believe it! Your dad and my dad helping out after all that happened," she said.

Karl beamed. "I wonder what happened...he was really burned up."

Christine leaned toward him and planted a kiss gently on his cheek. "Let's hope Bustah and Bumpah make it okay, that's really all that matters now."

"I wonder," said Karl, a frown furrowing his brow.

"Now what else could happen?" Christine said, puzzled.

"Oh, I don't know. The Greenfields and Tripper aren't going to be too happy after all that's happened...and then to have the Coast Guard board Tripper's dad's boat...I mean...that didn't sit too well. I don't think it's all over—not by a long shot."

"But Tripper had a rifle. He got what was coming to him. He even had to toss his rifle overboard, and then the Greenfields lost their Robin Hood outfits, too," Christine said with a chuckle.

Some of the fleet had already trimmed sail catching a fairly strong blow from the southwest. They formed a V and headed toward Mollusk Point Lighthouse. Laughter and encouraging yells rose amid the fleet wrestling to steal the breeze from each other.

They were still sitting happily across from each other as the *Clamshell* rose and fell, sending a wash of foam back into the cockpit. Christine had the helm in one hand, and the sheet for the boom in the other, as they followed the rest of the fleet between the lighthouse and rocks into Mollusk Point Cove.

"They've gone," Christine said, gripping Karl's hand tighter. "Gone."

Tears formed in the corners of her warm steel blue eyes as Karl took both her hands in his, shaking his head slowly.

"I know," he said. He gently patted Christine's hands and climbed into the stern.

"Come on, mate," he cried. "Let's make haste for port," he said turning his head toward the wind allowing the breeze and spray to wipe his cheeks.

Quickly, Christine hauled in the jib sheet as Karl swung the tiller, turning, and headed past Mollusk Point Lighthouse.

The whole fleet swung around the red buoy, sharing the strong southwesterly breeze. Bows rose and slapped against the frothing blue water. White, red, and blue sails snapped tight, red telltale streamers blew straight out as the skippers called across the water to each other.

Christine joined Karl in the stern. "They're safe," she said, "safe, as long they stay out of the harbors..."

"...and the pool," Karl added.

They kissed.

Back at the docks, the flotilla crews were tying up, reefing sails, and noisily jesting with each other over the day's events.

Chauncey Philpot, however, was in a quandary.

"I'll never be able to figure this out," he said to Mrs. Marlene Dodds Robinson, a summer resident seated next to him on the dock.

"It's a wash, Chauncey," she said.

"But what will I tell the newspapers?" he said.

"Tell 'em Bustah and Bumpah won," Tiny Stinson said in his deep barrel voice.

Chauncey Philpot recoiled.

"What?"

"And, who might they be? Tourists?" Marlene Dodds Robinson said, shaking her head in disgust.

"Whales," Chauncey Philpot said dejectedly.

"Ooh, what are you talking about—how ridiculous! What do you mean, young man?"

"Oh, they're whales…we've been having quite a problem here just before you arrived, Mrs. Robinson."

"Chauncey…are you alright?"

"He should have explained it bettah…they're Bustah and Bumpah Beluga," Tiny Stinson said, his face swathed in a big grin. "They're a couple of whales who missed the St. Lawrence Seaway," he said.

"Beluga…Beluga…? Where in the world do they live?" a surprised Mrs. Robinson said, clutching Chauncey Philpot's wrist.

Stinson walked away chuckling as Chauncey Philpot tried to explain all that happened to a very puzzled Marlene Dodds Robinson.

27

An Empty Pool

A buoyant flock of happy sailors charged noisily across Quarry Cove Bridge and swarmed around Johnny's lunch truck. Like an old fairground Hurdy Gurdy, *Yankee Doodle Dandy* rolled forth from the metal speaker atop Johnny's wagon. But it was playing to an empty parking lot.

A few cars drifted aimlessly into the lot slowly panning the pool as they drove past the wagon. Seeing no activity, they eased back onto 1A and left.

"Where are the whales?" one curious Connecticut driver asked, as his wife and kids leaned anxiously forward.

"They left this morning," Tiny Stinson said, sauntering over to the car.

"We've driven up here specially to see them," the driver said, as his wife drew back, shoulders slumped while the kids moaned.

"Sorry 'bout that," Tiny said. "We had to get 'em outta here, and fast."

The man looked puzzled.

"Some people were ready to do 'em bodily harm," Tiny half-whispered to the driver, as his wife leaned forward and the kids in the back seat strained to hear.

"Hurt the whales, daddy?" the little girl said.

"No…no," Tiny said. "They're safe, honey. We took them home."

Tiny sniffed and turned away.

Johnny lost no time popping hamburgers into buns and hot dogs into rolls as he bantered back and forth.

"Too bad them whales are gone. I was doing the finest kind of business with them here." Johnny said as his griddle sizzled with the pungent flavor of hotdogs and eye-watering onions.

"I know where they went," Karl said.

Johnny quickly looked up.

"But I can't tell ya, 'cause I love the whales almost more than I love your hot dogs."

"Well, as long as they're safe…that's all that matters. They were good business for me, though, that's for sure," he said, wiping his hands on his apron, and whistling carefree along with *Yankee Doodle*.

"If all goes well…and I don't know why it shouldn't…they should be off the Gulf of Maine pretty doggone soon," Karl said.

"That means Bar Harbor vendors will get the business, once people hear there are whales offshore."

"Yes, why don't you go over there, Johnny?" Christine said.

Then everything went quiet. It was one of those silences brought on by an unexpected happening. *Yankee Doodle* piped away uninterruptedly from atop Johnny's canteen van, but everything else suddenly went dead quiet.

All eyes turned and narrowed on a long, sleek, black Cadillac with the top down. Larry Greenfield was behind the wheel, and a bob of blonde hair towered over the windshield in the seat beside him.

There was a hum of excitement as Tripper vaulted over the car door into the crowd, pushing past everyone. He strode determined up to Karl, where he halted and thrust his jaw forward.

"You think you're pretty damned smart, don't cha?" He drew back his right and swung, as Karl ducked and fell to his knees, then thrust his right fist at the inside of Tripper's left knee. Knocked off balance, Tripper was sent sprawling, banging his head into the wagon. Half-dazed, his body was twisted, with legs straight out. He looked completely confused.

139

The crowd responded with a roar of laughter, and someone said, "Whoo—how to go, Karl."

Tiny Stinson walked from around the back of the wagon and dumped an icy bucket of water over Tripper's head, and the crowd let out uproarious laughter.

Tripper jumped to his feet, shaking, he slapped his hands at his drenched jeans and t-shirt as he ran to his car. A cloud of dust swept the parking lot as Larry Greenfield floored the accelerator and almost flew onto Route 1A, just as Joe Mullins' police cruiser swung into traffic from Dingle's Rock.

Joe Mullins put the red bubble flasher on the cruiser's roof in spin as the siren started to wail. He flipped his cigarette through the window, turned the cruiser around, and gave chase.

The crowd roared its approval.

"Pretty slick," Christine said. "You'll have to show me how to do that."

"Yeah, Karl, where'd ya pick that up?" Tiny Stinson said. "I'll have to watch it around you from now on."

Karl finished his second hot dog, smiling, and shrugged his shoulders.

"Dad showed me."

They clustered around a picnic table, laughing and eating, and talking Beluga whales. That is, until Christine made a suggestion that they see a movie.

"They're showing the movie they made on Vinalhaven, *Deep Waters*," Tiny Stinson said. "Great show…seen it twice, and it's still good."

28

Dousing the Light

Karl's mom drove the Packard with Karl, Christine and three more pals in the back seat. Tiny's dad took his Studebaker with another five kids in it. Others joined in the procession of cars to Bangor and then joined the long line waiting outside the Bijou on Exchange Street.

After the movie, they settled for hot dogs and sodas at Izzy's across the street from the Bijou. Since sea water ran through their veins, the movie became the main topic of conversation—the boats, the language, and the story.

"A Maine writer wrote the original story," Christine said, her lips frosted with a chocolate milk shake.

"Yeah. She lives in Southwest Harbor," Tiny Stinson said.

"Ruth Moore," Shirley Boyington said. "And, it was called *Spoonhandle*.

"How do you guys know all this stuff?" Karl asked, biting into a hot dog.

"Who cares? I liked Dana Andrews," Shirley Boyington said, raising her eyebrows with a wicked wink.

"Dean Stockwell is real cute," Christine said, her tongue licking the chocolate malt from her lips, as she turned to Karl. "Well? Who did you like? Jean Peters?"

Karl shrugged his shoulders and pursed his lips. "Hmm," he paused. Then suddenly he spilled out – "The boats. I recognized some of them from stopping over at Quarry Cove." Christine and Shirley Boyington let out an "ugh."

The ride down 1A was just as noisy as the ride the other way. Everyone was gabbing away about the movie, and about school, but ultimately returning to Bustah and Bumpah.

"Wonder where they are…" Christine said. "I really miss them."

"They're having the time of their lives," Karl's mom replied.

"And, what about Nettie? I mean…do you suppose she's back, yet?"

"I hope so," said Karl. "That daylight switch has been acting up, lately. So I know she wants to be there to make sure the light comes on…or else, she's in trouble."

"So much better with just a regular switch," Christine said.

"I know it was giving her a bit of trouble. But I think she got it fixed," Karl said. "This would be the worst night to have that thing go on the blink."

"You're right, just look at the fog," Christine said. "Well anyway, we can check it once we get there. Not too much to worry about."

"I don't know about that," Karl said. "So much has happened this past week, I wouldn't be surprised to see the whales back in the pool."

"That's all we need. Had enough of that for now," Laura Bunker said, as she strained to see ahead.

The Packard's lights bounced back from an impenetrable thick wall of fog, and Laura Bunker hit the brakes quickly. "It's a real pea soup," she said, gripping the wheel and staring hard over the dashboard. "I hope Seth and the rest of 'em are alright. I can't imagine them making much headway in this."

The Packard plunged down a steep hill just past Winterport into a thick mass of grayish fog that hung like a thick curtain across the highway.

Laura Bunker let out an "Ooh," and hit the brakes. For a second everything was quiet. Shaking her head, Laura eased the car forward.

"Let me drive, mom," Karl said.

"You don't have your license yet. That's all we'd need, after what we've been through."

Laura Bunker slowly threaded the Packard down the curving hill as Christine and Karl stared hard ahead, trying to pick up a telltale bush, a sign, anything as a guide.

"Good thing they painted that white strip on the side of the road – or else," Laura Bunker said, straining to see through the thick gray blanket of twirling mist. The car was barely crawling, as she swung the car around corners, down dips, and up and over the many hills on the coastal route. A few cars headed in the opposite direction were bumper to bumper. One car's fuzzy headlights trailed behind them.

"Come on...come on...where are you...Quarry Cove?" Christine nervously mumbled, her chin resting on the dashboard, eyes trying to cut through the fog. "There it is," Christine cried out. Laura Bunker tapped the brakes. "We're here," Christine excitedly shouted brushing Karl's shoulders. "I just saw the Quarry Cove sign."

"Well, thank the Lord for that," Laura Bunker said, rolling her stiff neck briefly, before leaning forward over the top of the steering wheel

"Look at that," Christine said. "Nine o'clock. It's taken us an hour...it's usually, only thirty minutes," Christine said.

"I'm a slow driver...always have been...always will be...right, Karl?" Laura Bunker said. "But anyway, here we are." Jubilantly, she rolled down her window and thrust her arm out to make a left turn onto the Quarry Cove Bridge.

"Hey mom, look out!" Karl cried out, and everyone braced.

Laura Bunker quickly swung the car over to the left and braked as a car with no lights on shot out of the fog and clipped the rear fender. She angrily laid down on the horn, as Karl and Christine strained through the curtain of fog trying to see the vehicle.

"You crazy bum," Laura shouted. "Whew, that was some close call. Who in their right mind would be driving that fast in this pea soup, and with no lights on, mind ya."

"Some close call? Mom, he hit us," Karl said.

"You alright?" Laura Bunker asked.

"I thought we'd had it," Christine said, as Laura eased the car into first gear and headed for the hill.

"Too close for me," Karl said. "It doesn't make sense…"

"Obviously the driver had none," Christine said, as Laura Bunker slowed crossing the bridge.

Christine and Karl rolled down their windows anxiously staring in the general direction of where they thought Mollusk Point was.

"We'd never see it from here, anyway," Karl said. "It only swings in a forty-five-degree arc…and in this fog…forget it."

"It's not on…it's off," Christine said.

Karl's mom came to a quick halt. Christine quickly left the car, with Karl close behind her, as the other two kids sat there.

"What are you going to do?" Karl's mom said.

"Dunno…until we find out what happened," Karl said, closing the door.

"Let me drive you…it's too foggy to walk."

"Too foggy to drive, Mom…you might go into the swamp," Karl shouted back.

"Come on," Karl said. "We don't have a minute to lose. Let's go."

"Watch your steps along that path," Karl's mom yelled down the hill, as the two disappeared into the fog.

"Stay close," Karl said, trying to stay up with Christine as she raced past him.

"It's not on…I know…I can tell," she said. "Come on, we don't have a minute to lose." Only the heels of her white sneakers were visible, accompanied by the crunch of gravel as Karl tried breathlessly to keep up.

Christine was already in Nettie's kitchen when Karl took the last two steps up to the porch.

For a second or two his fingers clasped the windowsill as he peered through the kitchen window at the base of the peppermint-striped lighthouse. Only the lower quarter could be seen. The rest disappeared into a swirling wet shroud of mist just above the first window adjoining the spiral staircase. Dragger's deep-throated horns moaned back across The Reach, as though lost. Christine and Karl searched each other's faces for a word...some direction.

Even the ghostly and somber clang-clang tolling of the big red buoy just off the cove's entrance, or the fog horns at sea, could not penetrate the eerie and frightening silence that held the two in its grasp.

"How can Nettie live here, alone?" Karl said, staring desperately into Christine's taut face.

"Not for me...that's for sure. But c'mon, let's do something...and fast."

Both leapt up the last few steps and raced across the kitchen into the wooden passageway which connected the house to the lighthouse.

"Do you know how to start it?" Christine asked, as their sneakers slapped into the concrete walkway.

"I dunno."

"Think... C'mon...you can't think," Christine said. "Where is it?"

Christine followed Karl as he jumped inside the base of the lighthouse and dashed across the damp concrete floor to the black spiral staircase. Christine flipped on a light.

"What a creepy place this is at night," she said, her voice echoing around the tower.

Their breath trailed like smoke as Christine followed Karl up and around the bending stairway. Within minutes they reached the watch and service room just below the lantern room.

Quickly Christine raced across the wooden floor. Her sneakers slapped like a hand clap as she half ran to the wall clogged with switches, pipes, and electrical wires. "This is it," Christine said, after scanning the whole board. "It has to be." Nervously she pressed a red thumb-sized emergency button.

Nothing happened. She pressed it again, as Karl anxiously watched. Christine's head trembled with agitation.

"Come on…come on," she growled, jabbing her thumb on the button and letting out an "ouch," then shaking her sore thumb.

"Here, let me try," Karl said, moving forward.

"It's okay…I've got it," Christine snapped. "I'll get it yet."

"You girls…y'all the same," Karl said, as Christine chuckled and jabbed the button again.

There was a *whirr*, a slow curdling ghostly *whirr* above them. Christine lifted her finger, as she and Karl both stared up above at the ceiling where the sound came from. Christine clung to Karl's arm.

"What's that?" she asked suspiciously. She tightened her grip on Karl's arm as the *whirr* deepened into a rising growl. Metallic clicks, and clangs accompanied the growl, which softened into a purring sound. Christine jumped back, as a motor kicked into action and giant rods, gears and wheels whirred and clicked behind her.

"Karl!" she said, as they both stood stunned. A bright flash of white light swept across the narrow window overlooking the sea. The whole lighthouse was now pleasantly gurgling and whining, as diesel motors, gears and wheels jumped into action. There were squeaks and groans as metal pushed by diesel power started to turn the light behind huge, highly polished Fresnel lenses above them.

"It's on," Christine said, jumping up, grabbing Karl's forearm. He studied a panel of switches mounted on a board, with heavy black, green and red wires snaking along the wall up into the light tower.

"You did it," Karl said. "You did it…first shot, too. How'd you know what switch it was?"

"It said 'On'," Christine said, unable to withhold a smile, as she rushed with Karl to the window overlooking the Reach.

Their laughter filled the room as they hugged and happily peered through the narrow window to see the blinding white light cut a tunnel of light through the fog. They stayed there for what seemed hours, constantly checking the light. Then, standing together, they listened and chuckled at the weird noises of the gears, cogs and chains.

"Smarty pants," Karl said, as Christine chuckled. "Last one down's a weirdo." Letting out a wild hollow wolfman's wail, he took the spiral steps two at a time, with Christine close behind him.

Back in Nettie's kitchen, Christine found a notepad atop the *Lighthouse Keeper's Log*, which Nettie had left on the roll top desk across from the sink.

"Look at this," she said, her finger tracing an entry in the log."

"June 27, 1950, 0:600 hrs. Checked Fresnel lenses, cleaned lantern room. All systems working, but daylight switch seems slow. Notified CG Cmd.—Will send maintenance crew – N. Beal, USCG Lighthouse Keeper, Mollusk Pt. Station #12."

"Boy, she sure knows her job," Karl said. "So, the switch must have failed then, after all."

"You write it," Karl said, dropping the notebook in front of Christine. "She'd never be able to understand my writing."

Christine started to print a note in block letters similar to Nettie's entries in the log.

"How's this?" she said. "Dear Nettie, we turned the light back on as soon as we arrived back from the movies, at about— what time, Karl?"

"Do you have to bother with that?"

"Of course, we do. It had to be about nine o'clock...didn't it?"

"Right. Didn't you say it was nine when we reached the bridge? So, it took about five minutes to get here...and, it was back on at nine ten, not much later...I bet."

Christine put the note on top of the log and placed a salt shaker on it.

"I bet no one knew it was out," Karl said.

"I bet you're wrong," Christine said.

Leisurely, they strolled back along the fogged-in causeway to Quarry Cove, every few steps turning and checking to make sure the light's cone was sweeping across the Reach. Then Karl broke away.

"Where're you going? What's up?" Christine said, catching up with him, as he strode toward the spidery slate gray etchings of the black cobwebbed bridge. Christine trotted along with him.

"Was around here...wasn't it?" Karl said, as Christine clung to his forearm.

"What are you looking for?"

"Just a chance he left something behind...it was a pretty good whack we got."

Christine let go of his arm when she saw something at the end of the bridge.

"Here...Karl...here, take a look." She held up a piece of shiny metal, which Karl took from her.

"A side mirror...it's a mirror off the side of the car that struck us," he said.

Christine took it back and looked at it.

"Came off a big car, wouldn't you say?"

"Must have...did you get a chance to see it?

She shook her head. "It was just a foggy, big gray ghost," she said, as Karl looked over the chrome mirror, weighing it in his hands. "He didn't even have his lights on."

"You don't think...?"

"I bet you ten to one the driver of that car turned off the light," Christine said, nervously grabbing Karl and turning him to face her.

"You don't think the light failed on its own?" Karl asked.

"Could have...but...but why was this car in such a hurry to leave this place?"

"But who'd do such a crazy thing? I mean…well, if someone did, they could have caused a shipwreck. So who'd do such a stupid thing…and, why?"

They both looked up from the lamp and stared into each other's faces.

"No," said Karl looking at the solemn stare on Christine's face.

"Hmm, hmm," said Christine, her eyes narrowing. "Has to be…has to be."

"He never gives up," Karl said. "See what you did to him?"

The blue Packard was gouged along the rear right fender. The twisted and scratched mirror had flecks of blue paint on it, as best they could see in the bridge light, which hung like a marshmallow in the fog.

In the kitchen, Karl's mother turned the rearview mirror over as it lay on the kitchen table. She pushed it around with a finger, and hefted the weight.

"Came off a big car…ya got that right…a Caddy or Lincoln, or even a Hudson," she said, laying the piece back on the table. "Not too many of them around these parts…must have been a tourist…no one from around here would drive that fast in this fog." Christine and Karl shared knowing looks with each other.

Slowly, Laura Bunker steered the Packard across 1A and along the lake drive to Christine's home in Peppermill Cove. A worried and very concerned Mrs. Alley ran down the brick path to the car.

"Dad isn't back, yet," she said, giving Christine a hug.

"They should be alright, Molly," Karl's mom said. "They're in a good boat. That fog's thicker than any Afghan the Ladies Aid makes.

Clustered around the kitchen table, they chatted about the movie and the whale rescue. Molly Alley recounted a "flare-up" at the bridge after they had left. How the police chief almost had a heart attack, and how the boys with bows and arrows had to be chased away by "Your dad, Karl, and Christine's dad, too," she said. "It was some upset. But thankfully everything turned out alright." She stopped and looked at Christine and Karl, who were both grinning.

They jumped a little each time the Westminster clock on the fireplace mantle peeled out each quarter-hour, briefly diverting their attention from the week's events, and back to their concern for the men and Nettie, and the lateness of the hour.

Christine was slumped back in a large chair, the women sat on the sofa, and Karl was trying to stay awake listening to the barely audible radio when the phone rang, jolting them awake to stare hard at the phone sitting on a tiny table next to the front door. Molly Alley leapt to the phone.

"Yes, oh...good," Christine's mom sighed with relief. "Yes, that's fine. You think they'll be alright?"

Christine ran over to her mom as Karl and his mom stood up, all anxiously awaiting the news.

"Whew! They're okay," Christine's mom said, shaking her head with relief. "It was the Coast Guard at Southwest Harbor. They pulled in to let Nettie off so she could use the phone."

The phone rang again. It was Nettie wanting to speak to Christine or Karl.

"How are Bustah and Bumpah?" Christine said. "Oh, great."

"Yeah, they're okay, Christine...but, we have a problem...at least, I do," Nettie said. "We pulled into Southwest and the Coast Guard got a report that Mollusk Point light – my light was out...will ya do me a favor?"

"Don't worry, Karl and I took care of it...at least...we think we did."

Nettie sighed. "Oh...thank the Lord. We should be home within a couple hours...and thanks again...I love you two. See ya soon."

The fog still hung like a big thick gray blanket over Quarry Cove. Its long tresses were caught in the lighthouse swath of light, as it swirled along the causeway. Its wet shroud disintegrated through the tree branches. Like some ghostly aspiration it furled around the lower half of Mollusk Point Lighthouse. But it was no challenge to the broad shaft of powerful white light that coldly swept across The Narrows like a scythe.

"It's working, Mom. I wonder why it didn't come on," Karl said, as Laura Bunker drew the Packard up alongside their white clapboard home, threw the gear shift into first, and pulled on the hand brake. They both paused at the door and listened as the big red buoy off the Point tolled ominously, accompanied by the deep, mournful, and intermittent growl of the fog buoy between the islands.

"Brrr...who'd think it was June," Laura Bunker said, wringing her hands as she drew some water into a tea kettle and settled it on the end heater. Karl checked the gauge on the kerosene can, flipped it over and ran down the steps into the basement to refill it.

They drank tea as they sat waiting around the tiny round table. They kept looking toward the door, hoping to see it open and see Seth Bunker enter. After an hour, they both went to bed, but Karl couldn't sleep. He just sat on the edge of his bed staring toward the point watching the sonorous half sweep of the light, while listening to the monotonous moan of the fog horn and funereal tolling of the red buoy bell.

His head felt like an empty can. It clanged and banged as he tried to understand some of the week's events. Who would try to sink his dinghy? Who would turn off the light? Images of Tripper and the Greenfields with their rifles and arrows flashed across his mind. He could see them racing across the bridge. Tripper was raising his rifle at them on the bridge, and then again at them on the boat.

Although he hadn't thought too much about it after the Coast Guard arrived – it was still there – a haunting and frightening picture of someone gone mad. Then he felt a cold sweat cling to his body. He was shaking. His hands were shaking. He was scared. He gripped his fists and stood up. He was not afraid of

151

Tripper Gleason, or, anyone else. He'd take on any of them…any of them. He sat back on the bed. His mouth was trembling and his hands were still shaking.

Pushing the curtains aside, his eyes focused on the causeway. Except for quick jabs of faint light from the lighthouse, the causeway was buried in the fog. The steel cobwebbed bridge could just be seen beneath bridge lights.

He sat on the edge of the bed just staring at the bridge lights. He was frustrated. Unable to comprehend why another student would go to such extremes, even risking prison, and for what?

His head would jerk him awake as he sat there dozing. He focused on the bridge lights and just stared. Only the distant sound of bell and fog buoys floated back into the cove. Nothing moved. Even the fog appeared plastered across the window.

He rubbed his eyes. Something moved. He looked again down toward the bridge and fell forward on his knees by the window. A tall, dark, fuzzy shadow was moving slowly along the causeway, the beam of a flashlight swishing side to side. Karl shook his head. He was not seeing things – someone was down there. Someone was walking along the causeway looking for something.

His hand reached toward the bed and picked up the large chrome side mirror. Whomever it was he knew he had what they were looking for.

That person could only be none other than Tripper Gleason. He stood up and the mirror slipped out of his hand clanging on the wooden floorboards.

"Damn," he cried out. The waving flashlight beam on the causeway stopped abruptly…but only for a brief second. The light went out. There was a scurrying of feet in gravel and then someone was running.

Quickly, he dashed downstairs. It was almost four o'clock when he heard a car start up at the far end of the bridge. Straining around the front door, he could just make out a quick flash of brake lights as a car sped out onto 1A and dissolved in the fog.

29

Narrowing the Gap

"Goin' ta sleep all day? What's the matter? Can't take it?"

"Dad—hey, you made it back okay, then?" Karl sat up shaking his head and rubbing his eyes as he jumped off the bed and stared at his father standing with his feet apart in his thick red-ringed stockings by the door.

"Finest kind," his dad replied, with a laugh. "Bit slow…seen some fogs, but this one was a beaut."

Gray whiskers of the ghostly fog coiled across The Narrows, as a fierce red sun—a huge steaming globe— majestically eased itself out of the ocean, the gulls screeching a welcome as they soared across a robin's-egg blue cloudless sky.

Warmed by hot coffee, their stomachs filled with pancakes, their tongues still honey-sweet with Maine maple syrup, father and son, together, strode happily down the little hill toward their boat, their black lunch pails slapping against their hip boots.

"A-ya Seth?" Chuddy Spooner's raspy voice sang out as he swung down the boat house ramp dropping his paint mask onto his multi-colored paint-sprayed coveralls. Seth turned and stopped.

"What in the name of thundah's goin' on? Everyone's losing their minds, or going crazy!"

"Why, what's up?" Seth said, as the burly, paint-speckled man drew level.

"Big trouble down yonder," he said, nodding toward Mussel Point Lighthouse. Karl and his dad turned, just as a dark blue U.S. Coast Guard sedan stopped in front of the lighthouse.

"Understand someone almost went aground last night, 'cause Nettie forgot to turn on the light an'…"

"That's a lie," Karl said, and his dad raised his hand to check him.

"It's an automatic light, Chuddy. So, I don't understand, and—"

"Heard Nettie was out messing with whales…that's why. She ought to get fired, after all we done for her."

"Best get your story right, Chuddy. From what I heard, she's been having a lot of trouble with that switch," Seth Bunker said.

"Well, that's all I hear…an' it don't look good fer her."

"Why?" Karl asked, as Chuddy Spooner, wiped his hands on a paint-smeared rag, and turned. "Why…what's going to happen?" Karl said.

"Find out t'night, I guess. They're meeting at the school house," Chuddy Spooner said, walking back up the short wooden ramp into his boat house.

Karl started to walk after him, but his father caught his elbow. "Come on, we'll take care of that later."

The *Laura* sailed smoothly through calm waters past the lighthouse, its powerful diesel engine whirring contentedly below deck as it left a black rope of smoke over the cuddy. Karl stood amidships, staring at the lighthouse and the porch where Nettie could usually be seen sweeping off the steps and tending her window boxes. But it was unsettling. The door to the house and post office—which would normally be open—was closed. The dark blue official-looking sedan with its long black antenna on the trunk sat ominously in front of the keeper's cottage. Karl's neck stiffened and his stomach tightened as he imagined the worst was about to happen.

"Come on, let's haul," his dad called, swinging the *Laura* toward The Narrows. Karl thrust his hands into a bait barrel – a soupy brown mixture of herring fish heads and tails– scooped up a handful and tossed them over the stern. There was a chorus of delighted high-pitched screams as the gulls nosedived into the sea, some grabbing a bite, others fiercely batting their wings and charging after those luckier than they.

155

Around eleven, his dad hooked a buoy, looped the rope over the winch, pulled the brown paper bag across the console, and foraged inside for bread and some cans of sardines. Together, with seagulls screeching and the boat tugging lazily at the mooring, they munched into Spurling's Bakery Finest Sliced Bread and cans of Alley's sardines.

"Here, have another, you look starved," his dad said, nodding at the can. "You should like them…look who canned 'em," he said, raising his eyebrows and chuckling. Karl opened the can of Alley's Finest Atlantic Sardines in Oil and made short work of the tiny herring along with two more slices of bread, before tucking the cans back into the paper bag and dropping them onto the bunk inside the cabin, where the diesel lolled.

"Does she like 'em?"

"Christine? Oh, I guess not. She can't even stand clams," Karl said, as his dad chuckled.

"So, what happened, Dad?" Karl ventured, as his father rested on two elbows staring out to sea, as he silently chewed and took a drink of coffee from his flask.

"About them whales…? It went too far. About the time I saw that Gleason kid with a rifle and them Greenfield boys with their bows and arrows, I decided something had to be done," he said, biting into a round of bread and fishing a sardine out of the can.

"But what about the Chief?" Karl said.

"Woody Harrington? Wouldn't know enough to come in out of the rain…and…an' lockin' Nettie up in his shed…," he started to chuckle, "if that don't take the cake…nothin' will."

"But I thought you didn't like Nettie?" Karl said.

"Never said that…jest didn't like the way she encourages those whales into the pool."

"But they came on their own…no one asked them to come."

"That's as much as you know. She had some other whales up there some years back when Phil was around…good man, her Phil. Had to talk her into not feeding them and encouraging them to stay…with all that coodle-ooh-la-hoola hoopla she puts out…might have thought she'd slipped a ring."

Hungrily, he took a herring off his fork and bit into a slice of bread. As he finished his last can of sardines, he pushed it into the brown paper bag along with the bread wrapper and Karl's empties, and passed it to Karl, who chuckled and tossed it below deck on the bunk.

"But like a fella says…it went too far…way too far. Wonder someone didn't get hurt. You're okay, aren't ya?"

"Thanks, Dad," Karl said. He wanted to reach out and clasp his dad's arm, to hug him and tell him how much he lov…liked him. But he couldn't. Men just don't do those things.

"I only did what I thought was necessary. Mind you, I'm not a big fan of having whales in the pool…kinda cute little fellas though," he said with a smile. "Coast Guard fellas said it was unusual to have them type of whales around here. Nettie must have a special charm on 'em."

"Now we got that light business to handle. Nettie will be some lucky if she's got a house— let alone a job—by the end of the day," his dad said, munching away, a slight grin crinkling his nose.

"But Dad, it wasn't Nettie's fault, the light switch…that switch was on the blink," Karl said, looking imploringly at his father, who took one of the remaining cans of sardines and pushed it across the console toward Karl.

"Never heard of them switches breaking down," his dad said, as he uncoiled the buoy rope from around the hoist and slipped the boat into gear.

Karl winced.

"However, that's not to say it couldn't happen."

"Dad? It just didn't happen. That light was turned off…"

"What?"

"Christine and I both believe it was Tripper."

"By Gawd, that's a hell of a thing to say. If he did, he'll be cracking rocks down at Thomaston."

"He's mad about the whales and he's even madder with Nettie. He'd do anything to get rid of her," Karl said, as his father listened intently.

"Well…mind you I'm not saying he did. But if he did, or anyone else did for that matter, they sure picked one hell of a night to do it. Anyway, the Coast Guard will find out. Come on, we've got five more strings to do…then we can go tackle the rest of it."

They later unloaded one hundred pounds of lobster at Alley's busy lobster pound in Bluebeard's Cove in Pepper Mill. Seth Bunker finished watching over the weighing, then leaned into the gangway and walked into the office perched on the end of the wharf where he met Christine's dad.

30

The Truth is Almost Out

Karl enjoyed the warmth of a burning sun as he swabbed and flushed the deck down with buckets of sea water, after brushing away sea weed, crab shells, and kelp. He was standing on the stern when another boat bumped and rubbed up alongside. Stumbling, he quickly caught his balance and looked down at the grinning face of Chester Gleason, Tripper's dad.

"Almost took a spill, eh?" Chester said with a grated chuckle. "You folks are in for an even bigger one tonight when you see what they'll do to that whale lover." A scratchy, hoarse throat chuckle followed. He turned his head and spat bits of a wet chewed cigar over the gunwales. "Oh yeah, that Nettie sure got herself in a tangle over this one."

Karl leaned on his broom as the boats creaked, rubbing together.

"Maybe your son is in for a surprise, too," he said, staring hard at the father of the school football star.

"Ya can say what ya want about our Wilbur…"

Karl couldn't suppress a chuckle and let loose laughing hard.

"I say somethin' funny? He ain't done nothin'…"

"So, firing a rifle on the bridge and threatening to shoot us is nothin'?" Karl said.

"He didn't shoot nobody…he was just trying to get rid of all that pile of ugly whale fat b'fore it destroyed our fishing…b'sides, if he had fired at ya, ye wouldn't be here t'day, I can warrant that."

He spat out the remnants of a mushroom-ended cigar and prepared to ease off. Angrily, Karl dropped the broom and pail and jumped amidships.

"There's something else, too," he said, as Gleason slipped back into neutral. "Yeah," he said, and then caught himself.

"Like what? C'mon, let's hear it...like all them other lies you and that Alley girl spread about him."

"Mr. Gleason. Christine and I have never said anything about Trip—," he tried to hold back a laugh, "...eh, Wilbur, that we wouldn't say to his face."

"Oh, so what's the big deal...this somethin' else ya talkin' about?"

"You'll find out...you'll find out," Karl said, feeling a glow of victory push aside the chilly feeling he had all morning.

Gleason looked puzzled. "You'd better not be making up anything against my Wilbur," he said, as Karl chuckled. "Ya can laugh...I've a good mind to give ya a kick where Wilbur should a done a long time ago... b'sides, I ain't got no use for nobody who steals another man's girl."

"So, that's it," Karl said, as Gleason's boat roared and he leaned over the gunwale pushing it clear. "So, that's it...jealousy...jealousy."

But Gleason didn't hear him, as his thirty-foot *Wilbur Boy* showed her stern and ploughed out of the cove.

"*Wilbur Boy*," Karl cried out. He nearly doubled over in laughter as his dad and Christine's dad called to him.

He was still chuckling as he climbed the gangway and joined both men on the deck overlooking the cove as *Wilbur Boy* left a trail of black smoke around Morgan's Point.

"What's he doin' here?" Christine's dad said. "He told me he was through with me after the meeting—for being a traitor."

"Traitor?" Seth Bunker said, snorting with contempt. "Traitor? So where's he selling?"

"He's hauling 'em all the way to Billings' in Belfast...just an extra five miles on his engine and a little extra gas...for less than what he gets here...all because we disagree...a difference of opinion. Amazing what that does to people...eh, Seth?" he said, giving him a short, good-natured jab to his shoulder.

"I know...don't rub it in," Seth said, "but he'll probably disagree even more when we get through with tonight's mess."

"I still don't understand why that light failed to come on," Christine's dad said. "Of all nights to stop working...yet, Christine said it kicked right in when Karl pressed the switch.

"Christine found it and turned it back on...not me," Karl said. "But then, Nettie said she'd been having trouble with it. She'd told the Coast Guard and they were forever going to have someone check it out. But each time they called, they seemed satisfied that it was running okay."

Both men nodded their heads, as lobstermen unloaded lobsters below on the wooden storage pens, refueled their boats, and trekked past them to get paid.

"So what happened to that light?" Spider Hawkins said, grinning and bristling with excitement as he tapped his catch money into his wallet with a coil of trap rope looped over his forearm. The men shook their heads as Spider, a wiry former paratrooper who had jumped into Normandy on D-Day, put both hands on the gangway ladder and slid the thirty steps to the keep float.

"See ya tonight," he called back to them, as he untied his white-hulled, twenty-four footer *Rip Cord*, hopped aboard, and churned a wake between the incoming boats. Patti Page's melancholy *Tennessee Waltz* trailed dreamily back across the warm harbor from his Trans Am radio.

"I hope nothing happens to Nettie," Karl said, as his dad started toward the gangway.

"It's good she's got you and Christine on her side...you two are a...well, a two-man army," Christine's dad said, and clamped a hand on Karl's shoulder. "Let's see what happens tonight...right, Seth?"

The Coast Guard sedan was still outside Nettie's house as they maneuvered between the buoys with the tide on the ebb down the narrowing channel.

"Them whales sure must be happy," Seth said, as Karl hooked the mooring buoy. "No more mud...b'sides, we're happier too."

"I kinda miss 'em, Dad. They were...well, different, almost like having a pet cat or dog. They always seemed to be laughing...and then, singing."

"They sure did make some strange noises," his dad said. "And...well..."

"What?"

"Well, I don't know...sounds a bit crazy...but, ah, well, they seemed to know Nettie, and Nettie talked to them like she'd known 'em all her life. An' then she started that whoo-hoo-ahoo stuff an' I'll swear, them whales almost started to dance. Now don't you go tellin' anyone what I said, do ya hear?"

Karl felt a warm rush of satisfaction flood his body. He'd never heard his dad talk like this before. He was strictly a hard working red-blooded red-neck fisherman with no time to waste on sentimentality.

"Remember...and, no matter what happens tonight...you just forget what I said...'cause I'll have plenty to say, anyway."

He wanted to hug his dad, but the traditional wide emotional separation between father and son stopped him. His father looked at him a little surprised as Karl's face reflected his love.

"Good haul," he said. "Going for two dollars and twenty-five a pound, so we made out alright... as a fella' says."

"Finest kind," Karl said, as his dad laughed and patted his shoulders.

31

Facing The Truth

The six o'clock WBCF newscast told listeners about Bustah and Bumpah being resettled off Bar Harbor, and that the Peppermill and Quarry Cove fishermen would be meeting tonight to express their concerns about the Mollusk Point Lighthouse, which had failed during the recent fog.

The Peppermill High School gym was nearly crowded when Karl and his father arrived, recognized immediately by Wally Hadlock of WBCF, who rushed over, waving his mic. Karl scanned the gym anxiously looking for Christine.

"So, Mr. Bunker, what can you tell me about the meeting tonight?" Seth Bunker tried to edge past Hadlock, but the reporter persisted in questioning him. A photographer from the *Bangor Express* edged up and requested a picture, but Seth Bunker waved him away.

"Why don't you wait and see what happens, then I'll tell you something?" he said.

"But you helped escort the whales out to sea with Nettie Beal...and we thought you were angry with her...do you know what happened to the light? Why it didn't come on?"

"Mrs. Beal can probably answer those questions better than I. As for the light, the Coast Guard is here to find out. I sure as h...eck don't know."

Karl paced around outside the gym looking for Christine as the residents of Quarry Cove and Peppermill streamed into the gym. The parking lot was crammed with cars and trucks. He saw the same dark blue sedan with the long whip antenna on the trunk and the Coast Guard shield on the driver's door.

"Hey, fink."

Karl spun around. Tripper Gleason glared down at him. Three of his lackeys stood close by, grinning. He wore a large blue and white striped windbreaker, new sneakers, and looked even taller than his big-boned, six-foot frame.

"Tonight's the night you guys are going to wish you'd never heard of the Tripper, he said with a grin, pointing a skinny, long, right index finger a hair from Karl's nose. "Hope you've said your goodbyes to Nettie Beal?"

"Have you packed?" Karl swung around to face Christine.

Christine grabbed his forearm, a big smile across her face, as Tripper's face went gaunt.

"You better, 'cause you're in really...I mean...really, big doo-doo," Christine said, letting out a wild giggle. The two friends she came with laughed.

"Whadya mean, trouble? You're hanging around with trouble. I always liked you, Christine. I just can't understand why you'd bother with this jerk."

"Well, you never offered me a ring, did you?" Christine said, with big smile and laugh. She tightened her grip on Karl's arm, who looked as shocked as Tripper.

"What's all that about?" he asked, as they trouped into the gym. "A ring?"

"Don't worry, but it sure got his attention."

"And, what's this about him packing? Do you know something I should know?"

"I just wanted to kick-start his football brain-dead head into gear to see if he can still think," Christine said.

Chauncey Philpot, garbed as impeccably as ever, shuffled up to the podium amid the half-circle of speakers which included Coast Guard officers, school officials and Chief Harrington, who was seated at the far left of the Coast Guard.

"Good evening," he started. As some whistles punctuated his introduction, he blushed with embarrassment.

"This is a meeting concerning the operation of Mollusk Point Lighthouse…eh…which didn't come on the other night. I mean, the light failed to ignite…or…well, something happened…"

"Short of candles?" a male voice shouted, followed by uproarious laughter.

Chauncey lowered his head as Chief Harrington walked to the podium and whispered something to Chauncey as he retired to the chairs behind the podium.

"This is a serious matter," the Chief started. "We're not here to make fun about it. We're trying to find out what happened and—"

"Get a lighthouse keeper…" Tripper Gleason's voice rang out, accompanied by some twittering from his cronies.

The Chief brought the gavel down and glared at the source. "You'll get a chance to say your piece, Mr. Gleason, but let me say what I have to say and introduce you to our distinguished panel."

The crowd applauded.

"My son is only saying what a lot of us feel should be said," Tripper's dad said, leaning the full girth of his body over the chair and tilting Mabel Wandsworth's gull feather hat over her forehead. The tiny ninety-year-old quickly straightened it and glared at Chester Gleason who ignored her and kept on talking.

"That's enough," the Chief said, tapping the gavel. "Please remain seated and wait to be recognized."

Christine was twisting and turning in her seat trying to locate Nettie.

"Where is she? Surely she should be here…"

Karl's search for her also failed.

Coast Guard Commander Bruce Williams took the podium to a hearty round of applause and some whistles from Tripper and his cronies.

"What happened here is a rare…well—it just doesn't happen," he said. "We're regretful for the failure, but relieved that no tragedy occurred."

"The day switches have been working well…but, we were aware that something had happened at Mussel Point a month ago. Fortunately, our lighthouse keeper, Mrs. Beal, was on the job and able to rectify the problem. I believe—"

"Too busy taking care of whales…that's the problem. If she'd have been there, this would never have happened…and…an—"

Commander Williams pointed his finger at Tripper Gleason.

"I'd advise you to control your outbursts or leave the hall, sir."

"He's only saying what he has a right to…," Chester Gleason said, jumping to his feet.

"Then perhaps you'd like to continue your conversation with that gentleman outside?" Commander Williams said, as the crowd stomped their feet and applauded.

Chester Gleason sat down slowly, only to be accosted by Mabel Wandsworth, who angrily turned on him, wagging her finger, "Why don't you have the common decency to show some respect for these fine men in uniform who have come here tonight to help us solve this serious problem."

"Damn summer people," Chester Gleason mumbled, barely audible, as the crowd once again cheered, this time for Mabel Wandsworth.

"We plan to replace the day valve switch," Commander Williams went on. "In fact, it should have been replaced by our maintenance crew by now. Fortunately, no one suffered. It was an extremely foggy night and very dangerous. Most fishing vessels had already sought port and the lobster fishing boats had finished the day's work before the fog dropped."

The Commander then opened the floor for questions.

"That still doesn't explain the treacherous situation it left us in," Chester Gleason said as he stood up. "Just suppose someone was out late…"

"We have to deal with facts, sir, not supposition. We recognize the dangers."

166

"Yes, and this wouldn't have happened had we had a keeper who was maintaining the light…instead…she was taking care of two whales that threatened our fishing."

"Chester Gleason."

All eyes turned to the door. A confused mumble of voices stopped as Nettie Beal stood defiantly in the doorway, hands clasped below her waist, shaking her head.

"Yea, Nettie!" Karl and Christine chorused along with others. She waved to them and then, at the invitation of the commander, took the podium.

"My, my, what a horrible situation. I must apologize for the failure of the light not working. And yes, had I been there—like I am almost 24 hours a day—I probably would have caught that person or persons who snuck into the cottage, climbed the stairs to the maintenance room, and turned off the light with the emergency switch."

There was a hushed gasp and the assembly hall went silent. Everyone was staring at Nettie as her eyes swept the audience until they rested on Tripper Gleason. Without moving her focus and looking very tense, she waited.

Chester Gleason sprang to his feet. "Don't tell us you're accusing someone of turning off the light when you left your post to take care of the whales, and couldn't care less."

Nettie turned and looked toward the Commander behind her. He rose and walked to the podium.

"The light was not out for more than ten minutes, sir, from the time we got the call until it was restored," Commander Williams said, waiting for any response Gleason might have.

"It was out longer than that," Gleason said.

"Oh, and about what time did you notice it was out, sir?" Commander Williams said.

"Musta bin about eight forty…my son…eh, Wilbur, told me about it."

He nodded his head and looked at his son who glared back at him.

"He was on his way back from Belfast when he passed Quarry Cove an' could see it wasn't on."

"That's strange," the Commander said, looking back at a fellow officer. "We had no reports before then. But there was a dragger that reported the light working at nine as they passed through The Narrows, but suddenly it went off. I think that was at…"

He looked over his shoulder as a lieutenant picked up a file and walked to the podium.

"Ah, yes," he said, smoothing out the sheets of paper in the file. "The dragger *Hercules* reported that the Mollusk Point light was working until the light failed at 2100 hours…that's nine o'clock…and then…," he flipped the pages, "the dragger said the light came back on at 2110…that's ten minutes after nine."

The Commander looked up and stared at the Gleasons.

"Well, he could have been mistaken," Gleason mumbled, shuffling uncomfortably in his seat as Tripper's face flushed.

"So, do you remember what time it was when you called the Coast Guard station, Mr. Gleason?" the Commander asked.

Gleason wiggled around uncomfortably in his chair.

"Could it have been eight thirty?" the Commander said.

"How was I ta know? I just called to let the Coast Guard know the light was out," Gleason said awkwardly, as Tripper shuffled his feet and mumbled to his dad.

"That was at 2030…or, eight thirty, then. That's the time your call was recorded in the Coast Guard log," the Commander said, waiting for a reply.

Christine and Karl beamed at each other.

An angry Chester Gleason sat down heavily in his chair and started to argue with his son. "Ya' told me it was off at 8:30," Chester Gleason snarled. The commander looked surprised at his fellow officer.

"That's when I turned into the cove," Tripper could be heard, trying hard to muffle his voice. "It was about nine when I reached the light. It was so foggy."

"Dang' fool," his father shot back.

Nettie spoke briefly with the commander and he stepped back as she took the podium. "Amazing isn't it. The light was reported out thirty minutes before it went out. Now how d'you suppose that could happen? Clairvoyance?"

The audience groaned and swapped looks with each other. Chester Gleason and his son sat quiet, staring straight ahead.

"I don't want to point the finger at anyone…this is a very serious crime…a federal offense. But, I'm sure someone here tonight knows something about this," Nettie said. "That light didn't malfunction. Someone turned it off."

"Who was it, Nettie?" Christine called out, as others joined in. "Yea, who was it?"

The Gleason's suddenly rose and stalked out of the room. At the door, Chester Gleason turned. With a beet-red face, he started to wag his finger toward Nettie, who stared at him hard.

"Come on Chester. Why hold back. You've got nothing to hide…or, have you? Chester Gleason followed his son out of the building.

"I have an idea…actually more than just an idea…but for now I'll keep quiet. I believe I know what happened. But for now I'll keep quiet and let the Coast Guard continue its investigation," Nettie said.

"Bust 'em now, Nettie," Seth Bunker's deep voice cried out.

"Yeah, let him have it," said another.

Even Mabel Wandsworth cried out, "You should press charges, my dear…press charges."

"I'd like to thank two very wonderful young friends of mine," Nettie said, as the hum of the audience slowly went quiet. "These two—stand up—didn't wait for the alarm; they immediately ran to the light and fixed the problem post haste."

The audience turned and cheered as Christine and Karl awkwardly rose, and quickly sat down.

Commander Williams expressed the appreciation of the Coast Guard while people thronged around Nettie, Christine and Karl. Their dads walked over and expressed their support.

"Just one more item," the Commander said, as the crowd quieted down. "The Coast Guard is happy that no accidents occurred. This case is, however, of a very serious nature, and we will continue to investigate why this light failed. We will keep everyone informed of the outcome of this investigation."

The crowd applauded and cheered.

32

Just Off Bar Harbor

Nettie had a slew of photos of Bustah and Bumpah. She had picked them up from Sawyer's Drug Store in Belfast the Tuesday following all the excitement. Christine and Karl looked at them dozens of times as they had lunch with Nettie. As Karl ate Nettie's clam chowder and Christine ate a lettuce and tomato sandwich, she held up one photo of the two whales she wanted.

"I knew all along who did it," Nettie said, leaving the kitchen table and crossing to the window that overlooked The Narrows. For a while she just stood staring out beyond the bridge toward the open sea.

Christine and Karl walked over and linked their arms around Nettie's waist as Nettie looped her arms over their shoulders.

"I wonder where they are," she said. "What a week this has been. Who would have ever thought two whales could have caused so much happiness…and so much trouble?"

The trio climbed the stairwell into the gallery surrounding the light. She stared off into the distance, a splash of foam attracting her attention as Christine pointed out through The Narrows.

"Look…oh, now, it can't be!"

"It isn't, but don't fret…they'll be back. You can bet on that, just as sure as this light comes on every night," Nettie said with a contented smile. "Oh—and just as long as I have two of the best friends in the world to help me keep that promise."

That Wednesday, the *Bangor Express* reported that Wilbur "Tripper" Gleason of Pepper Mill Cove had been charged with malicious mischief in Waldo County Municipal Court. His father was also charged in a co-complaint. The charge was brought by Mrs. Laura Bunker, who presented the court with a side mirror which she claimed Tripper allegedly lost when he slammed into Mrs. Bunker's car on the night the light went out at Quarry Cove. Tripper pleaded guilty to the charge after police officer Joe Mullins produced evidence which included the light and a photograph of the damaged car. But the malicious mischief charges against Tripper and his father were dismissed for lack of evidence, and Tripper was fined fifty dollars for leaving the scene of an accident.

As the weeks trolled by, the residents of Quarry Cove returned to their normal life of fishing and attending church and town meetings. Chauncey Philpot was in full control. Chief Harrison and his wife moved on to Florida.

"Twenty-five years is enough," he told the *Bangor Express*, and almost exploded when an enterprising reporter asked whether he had been forced to resign because of the manner in which he handled the whales.

The Gleasons shunned the public light. Tripper quit football after the crowd booed him off the field. His father posted a For Sale sign on their home, and took off with a rental truck carrying their belongings. No one knew or knows their exact destination. Some said Portland. Others heard New Hampshire. There was just no peace after what had happened. Quarry Cove and Pepper Mill folk don't soon forget.

Then, one Saturday morning, with Seth Bunker behind the helm, the *Laura* chugged out of Quarry Cove into The Narrows, under The Reaches Bridge, and set a steady course about fifteen miles off Bar Harbor.

It was a cool fall day. Laura Bunker sat in the cuddy alongside Seth. Karl, Christine, and her dad and her mother, along with Nettie, lined the rail, waiting. They were about ten miles out to sea with Cadillac Mountain just a cone on the horizon, when Nettie lifted her head and stared across the ocean.

"Hool-a, hool-a, hupley," she warbled, much like a yodeler.

Christine gripped Karl's elbow as she stared across the blue patch of swells. An unusually large band of seagulls were squawking and screeching. Karl instinctively reached inside the bait barrel and fished out some sloppy herring bait and tossed it to the swarming birds.

The birds dived down over the swell, just as two large snouts popped up between the waves.

Clickety-click-clack...Clickety-click...clacker, clack.

"Come on, my babies," Nettie cried out. "Come on...back to momma," she called.

"Hool-a, hool-a-hoo..."

Tears ran freely down her cheeks as she scooped a double handful of herring bait and flung it toward the snouts of Bustah and Bumpah. The whales dove and surfaced, shot up fountains of water, then sang in moderate pitch, "Oo-ha...ooh..ah..."

Seth Bunker put the boat in neutral. He and his wife, Christine and her mom and dad, along with Karl and Nettie, watched excitedly as two exuberant whales rolled and cavorted just as though they were back in Quarry Cove pool.

Above a slight wash on the bow of the *Laura* a strange, mellow, soothing and haunting song floated above the swell. Everyone stood still, listening.

"It's like they're trying to tell us something," Seth Bunker said quietly, his head down, as he listened intently to the rhapsody of the whales. There were damp eyes and glowing faces. All turned and nodded in agreement.

Seth Bunker swallowed. A big smile crossed his ruddy complexion. Then he suddenly bowed his head and turned away. "Got t' check the engine," he said, and disappeared below.

About the Author

Ken Buckley loves writing. At 18, fresh from England, he lived on Cranberry Island where he first published with the *Ellsworth American* when he wasn't painting houses, shingling roofs, building fishing weirs, or baiting lobster traps. After serving with the Marines in Korea, he worked 32 years with the *Bangor Daily News*, and later, three small weeklies, including one of his own. Married with two grown children, he has one grandson. Family, sea, sailing and writing occupy his life.

www.ingramcontent.com/pod-product-compliance
Lightning Source LLC
Chambersburg PA
CBHW020651260626
47157CB00008B/2994